A note from the editor...

Well, this is it—the last month of Harlequin Temptation. We've had a good run, but everybody knows that all good things have to end sometime. And you have to admit, Temptation is very, *very* good....

When we celebrated our twentieth anniversary last year, we personified the series as a twenty-year-old woman. She was young, legal (well, almost) and old enough to get into trouble. Well, now that she's twenty-one and officially legal, she's leaving home. And she's going to be missed.

I'd like to take this opportunity to thank the countless number of authors who have given me, and other Harlequin Temptation editors past and present, so many hours of enjoyable reading. They made working at Harlequin an absolute pleasure.

I'd also like to thank our loyal readers for all their support over the past twenty-one years. Never forget—you are the reason we all do what we do. (Check out the back autograph section if you don't believe me.)

But this doesn't have to be the end....

Next month Harlequin Blaze increases to six books, and will be bringing the best of Harlequin Temptation along with it. Look for more books in THE WRONG BED, 24 HOURS and THE MIGHTY QUINNS miniseries. And don't miss Blazing new stories by your favorite Temptation authors. Drop in at tryblaze.com for details.

It's going to be a lot of fun. I hope you can join us.

Brenda Chin
Associate Senior Editor
Temptation/Blaze

W9-AXV-382

Cat had decided to seduce Dylan about one minute after she'd learned he was a drifter

Soon. Immediately. *Tonight.*

Actually, she'd been toying with the idea from the moment she'd met Dylan's stare across the crowded bar. Something had happened—something electrifying and emotional and completely unexpected. She wasn't sure why, but she hadn't been able to shake the feeling that this *thing* building between them was destined to happen. In that moment it had risen above the sexual want they'd been dancing around since Friday night and had suddenly become...more.

Thank heaven she hadn't told anybody else about her new plans for herself and her life, because they'd think her crazy. The truth about Dylan's situation might have made her run screaming in the opposite direction if she'd already succeeded in her transformation from the reckless Cat to the mature responsible one.

Luckily, that hadn't happened yet. Besides, a girl could take on only so much at once, right? Saying goodbye to the family bar, Temptation, was quite enough all by itself, without throwing virtual celibacy into the mix.

So for now, Cat Sheehan was going to enjoy the hell out of Temptation...and *temptation.* With a man who epitomized the word.

LESLIE KELLY
HER LAST TEMPTATION

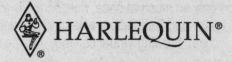

HARLEQUIN®

TORONTO • NEW YORK • LONDON
AMSTERDAM • PARIS • SYDNEY • HAMBURG
STOCKHOLM • ATHENS • TOKYO • MILAN • MADRID
PRAGUE • WARSAW • BUDAPEST • AUCKLAND

ISBN 0-373-69228-5

HER LAST TEMPTATION

This edition published by arrangement with Harlequin Books S.A.

® and TM are trademarks of the publisher. Trademarks indicated with
® are registered in the United States Patent and Trademark Office, the
Canadian Trade Marks Office and in other countries.

www.eHarlequin.com

Printed in U.S.A.

Dear Reader,

I hate saying goodbye. Whether it's hugging a loved one I seldom see after an all-too-brief visit or packing up my Christmas decorations wondering how the holidays could be over already—or even finishing a book populated by people I've come to care about—I find myself getting down with every farewell.

This one is especially tough. I love Harlequin Temptation, and knowing I won't be seeing those sassy red-covered books on the store shelves every month makes me very sad.

As a reader, I stumbled onto Harlequin Temptation back in the early nineties and read them avidly. So selling my very first book to my favorite line was a dream come true. I never imagined that a short six years later I'd be writing the last Temptation novel to be published in North America.

This book was truly a work of love. I and the other authors in this last month wanted to create a suitable tribute to the line that has sparked the careers of so many popular romance writers of today—and the line that has forged such a tight bond of friendship between its authors. So as you read the books, you might stumble across some familiar names...and yes, there are definitely some inside jokes. After all, Harlequin Temptation has always been about having fun and being just a little bit naughty.

I sincerely hope *Her Last Temptation* is worthy of standing beside all the marvelous Temptation stories that preceded it. And on behalf of all the Temptresses, thank you very much for your support and your enthusiasm. It's been a true pleasure entertaining you.

Best wishes always,

Leslie Kelly

To the Temptresses of the past who inspired me.
And to the Temptresses of today who have given me
some of the greatest friendships of my life.

Prologue

IF SOMEBODY STARTED singing that Little Orphan Annie song about the sun coming out tomorrow, Cat Sheehan was gonna hurl. Or run screaming into the street, pulling her hair out and kicking every road construction worker she came across right where it counted. Or maybe just wail to the sky, let the tears she'd never let drip from her eyes fall where they may, and face what she did not want to face.

Her uncertain future. Worse...the negation of her past.

She, her sister and their two best friends were practically alone in their bar, Temptation, shell-shocked by the letter they'd received from the historical society. Their plea to have their building designated a historical landmark— saving it from demolition by the city—had been rejected.

There was no sun. No tomorrow. Sure as hell no Daddy Warbucks. Nobody was coming to save them from the bureaucratic crime that allowed the city to shut them down after twenty-one years just because some newer businesses in higher tax brackets had enough clout to demand an unnecessary road widening.

"It's over," she said, still not believing it herself. "I knew those biddies from the historical society would reject us."

She hadn't really been talking to the others. More to the world in general, if for no other reason than to distribute some of the pain that had landed on her shoulders with a bit more equity.

Seeing everyone else looking at her, Cat busied herself behind the bar, making their signature drink, the Cosmopolitan. Cat and Laine had chosen it as a joke three years ago when they'd taken over the bar from their mom, because Kendall was about as uncosmopolitan as any dusty little Texas town could be.

It was only after she realized she'd forgotten to put any liquid in the shaker—which contained only ice—that she acknowledged how shaken up *she* was. She quickly corrected the situation, going heavy on the vodka.

Then, because everybody seemed to be waiting for her to say something—or else explode—she added quite mildly, she thought— "The city wants a new road, so we're out. Did you really think we'd change anything tonight?"

Passing out the drinks, she eyed the three other women, waiting for the "it'll be okays" to start. Laine appeared on the verge of tearing up; Gracie sighed, looking depressed rather than sad; and Tess seemed more nervous than anything else.

None of them looked the way Cat felt about the loss of this last fight to cling to a way of life her family had held dear for two decades—absolutely furious and utterly heartbroken.

Laine appeared close, however, at least as far as the heartbreak went. The sheen of moisture in her eyes cut deeply into Cat. Her sister never cried. She was the rock— the steady foundation of the family—and the antithesis of Cat. Her older-by-six-years sister was solid, smart and reliable. The calm one. The good one. The angel.

Solid, smart and reliable were three words that had never been used to describe Cat, the younger Sheehan sister. And nobody in his right mind had ever thought of her as good. Her blond hair and green eyes might appear angelic at first glance. But her attitude and never-ending ability to get into trouble had made her seem much more destined for a pitchfork than a halo as a kid.

Her adult life hadn't changed anybody's opinion.

She'd been called the rebel, the bad girl. Her mother had dubbed her the wild child at the age of three when she'd tried climbing headfirst out of her bedroom window to run away from home so she wouldn't have to start preschool. Laine had hauled her back inside by the laces of her Buster Browns that time.

But nothing was going to save Cat from falling now, especially not if Laine started showing emotion over this. Or worse, appearing helpless, as the slight tremble in her lip and the shakiness of the hand holding her martini glass indicated.

"How are we going to explain this to Mom?" Laine asked, sounding bewildered.

Laine at a loss? Unsure what to do? The sky was gonna start falling at any minute. And Cat just couldn't take it, not on top of everything else. So she raised a brow and gave her sibling a challenging look. "Had faith in the system, Laine, dear?"

Bingo. Her sister immediately stiffened. As usual, when Cat went on the offensive, she inspired rapid mood changes, often involving anger. Or sometimes laughter. She'd used the technique all her life and it was a damn good defense mechanism, if she did say so herself. Including now.

Laine's eyes darkened and her jaw tensed as she crumpled the letter in her hand. "Yes, I did. This isn't right. How can they just take away everything we've worked for?"

Cat nearly sighed in relief. A teed-off Laine, she could handle; a bereft one, she couldn't.

Everyone kept talking, but Cat couldn't bring herself to listen. The others all had a sad stake in this, but they weren't going to lose quite as much as she was. Her business, her job, her way of life. Even her home.

Okay, the three tiny rooms over the bar weren't much of a home, but they were *hers*. She loved retreating into her private little world, listening to the late-night whispers and creaks of the aged oak paneling downstairs as the old building settled ever deeper into its foundation. A foundation that had, until the city's road project, seemed incredibly sound.

The trill of birds in the lush walled garden right outside her window woke her every morning. And the tinkle of glasses and muted laughter of their regulars lulled her to sleep on her rare nights off. She loved those sounds. As much as she loved the smell of the lemony polish she used daily to bring back the lustrous shine to the surface of the old pitted bar.

She loved the hiss of a newly tapped keg. Loved the clink of glass on glass when she poured a neat whiskey. Even loved the whirr of the blender when she had to make girlie drinks for the froufrou crowd that occasionally wandered in for happy hour.

Mostly she loved sitting here, alone, late at night when the place was closed, picturing the faces and voices of everyone who had passed through here before her. Her grandparents. Her dad, who'd died so many years ago. She could still see his wide Irish smile as he slowly pulled a draft of Guinness for a customer, explaining that the nectar of Ireland was well worth the wait.

Gone. All the things she loved would be gone. Washed away, like sidewalk etchings in the rain, by city officials who had no idea they were washing Cat's entire world away, as well.

No job. No business. No home. No future.

No identity.

Just who was she going to be when this was all over?

She sipped her drink, depressed and overwhelmed at the thought. She'd gotten so used to her place in the world, stepping in at the bar at such a young age because it was what the family always figured she—the so-so student but A+ party girl—would do. She'd dated poor excuses for men and never been serious about any of them. Worst of all, she'd put away any glimmer of an idea that she could do something different with her life. Like fulfill a long-secret dream to go to college and become a teacher.

She'd shoved all of those things aside, and for what? A business that was going under, a family who had drifted apart, and a life that seemed…empty.

You can change it. Change everything.

She couldn't thrust the unexpected thought out of her mind…maybe she should take this as a sign to move on in a completely unexpected direction, to walk a new path.

She could change. Become somebody new.

The idea grew on her. Since she had no choice, maybe the time had come for her to try something else. To change some things about herself—from her attitude to her hairstyle. Her clothes to her social skills. She could work on her education—slowly—to see if she really would be as good at teaching English to teenagers as she thought she might be.

She could work on her notoriously bad language, her secret addiction to romance novels. Maybe she'd even break herself of her awful habit of getting involved with even-badder-than-herself bad boys, who were ever-so-safe to fall for since they never aroused any ridiculous expectations of happily-ever-after. Just happily-between-the-sheets.

Yeah. No bad boys.

"Who are you kidding?" she mumbled under her breath, doubting she was that frigging strong.

"Did you say something?" Tess asked.

Cat merely smiled, trying to tune back in on the animated conversation the others had been having. "Just talking to myself," she admitted. "Making some plans."

Plans. Yes, she definitely had to make plans. She had time—until the end of the month, at least. Her sister and two closest friends would be right here by her side for every minute of it, riding things out until the very end. They'd be like the string quartet on the *Titanic*, playing their instruments as the ship sank beneath their feet.

She'd use these last weeks to figure out how to become the new Cat Sheehan. Heck, maybe she'd even start going by Catherine. It was something, anyway, along with those other big changes, which she went over again in her mind.

Education. *Check.* Home. *Check.* Attitude. *Check.*

No dangerous men. *Hmm...*

But hey, stranger things had happened. All it would take was willpower. Well, that and the knowledge that no hot-enough-to-melt-a-polar-icecap man with trouble in his eyes and wickedness in his smile had wandered into her world in quite some time.

And one sure as hell wasn't likely to now.

1

SIN HAD JUST WALKED INTO her bar and he was wearing a Grateful Dead T-shirt.

Cat Sheehan paused midsentence, forgetting the conversation she'd been having with one of her customers. Forgetting *everything*. Because, Holy Mother Mary, a man who'd instantly set her heart pounding and her pulse racing was standing a few yards away, completely oblivious to her shocked stare.

He was tall. Very tall. And he had the kind of presence that immediately drew the attention of every person in the place—at least, every *female* person. Their gazes drifted over because of his size. They stayed because of his looks.

A strip of leather kept the man's jet-black hair tied at the back of his neck in a short ponytail. A simple thing, that piece of leather, and she'd certainly seen men with longish hair and ponytails. But on him, well, the look was…rakish. That was the only word she could think of.

Cat liked rakes. Not that she'd ever met one for real, but she liked the ones she'd read about in her pirate romance novels.

A pirate. It fit. From the ponytail to the flash of silver glistening on the lobe of one ear to the aura of danger oozing from his body, this man had the pirate thing going in spades.

His classically handsome face was lean, a faint shadow

of stubble adding a layer of ruggedness to his strong jaw. His lips briefly widened into a smile as he greeted some-one. For a moment, Cat felt very sure the ground had trem-bled a bit under the power of his smile. Not to mention the mouth, which looked as if it had been created for the sole purpose of kissing.

His body was a living testament to the beauty of na-ture—broad at the shoulders, slim at the hips, with long legs covered in tight, faded jeans. His thick arms flexed, muscles bulging under the weight of the sizable guitar case he was carrying, though he hardly seemed to notice. Lifting it higher, he stepped deftly around tables and chairs, skirting the outstretched legs of the few patrons in the place.

He moved gracefully. Catlike.

"Oh, yeah," she murmured. Cat *definitely* liked.

She never took her eyes off him as he approached. Then it sunk in. He was approaching *her*, Cat Sheehan, the woman standing here with her mouth only slightly less wide-open than her eyes.

Blinking, she gave her head a hard shake, then grabbed the nearest cloth she could reach and busied herself by wiping up some spilled beer.

"Hey! What are you doing?"

Cat barely registered the shrill words from somewhere nearby, because suddenly *he* was there. A thick, tanned forearm dropped to the surface of the bar, and she couldn't help staring at his fingers. Long fingers. Artistic-looking. Perfect for a guitar player. Not to mention a lover.

"Wow," the same female voice said, sounding subdued.

Swallowing hard, Cat slowly shifted her gaze, survey-ing his limb from fingertip to elbow, then the ninety-de-gree turn up the thick planes of his arm, the tight hem of the black cotton T-shirt. The broad shoulder. The hollow of his throat. The cords of his neck. *Wow, indeed.*

Then, oh, God, the face.

If Helen's face had launched a thousand ships to the sea, surely this man's could inspire *ten* thousand pairs of panties to drop to the floor.

Her legs wobbled, her knees knocking together loud enough to be heard over the sound of the jackhammer outside. But probably *not* loud enough to be heard over the pounding of her heart. Ordering herself to calm down, she slowed her breaths, mentally grabbing for control as she assessed the situation.

She was facing the most incredible man she'd ever seen—the kind of guy women fantasized about meeting for real, instead of on the pages of books or on giant screens in darkened movie theaters. One-hundred-percent pure sin.

Separating them were only the broad mahogany bar and Cat's own resolution to change her ways and steer clear of sexy, dangerous men.

She should have known she didn't have a snowball's chance of keeping that resolution, though, honestly, she'd figured she could last a week. But no. It'd been only three days since they'd received the letter from the historical society and she'd made the stupid promise to herself. Of all the changes in her world since Tuesday—including the shockingly abrupt departure of Laine and Tess for far-flung adventures—she'd thought the ones she'd resolved to make in herself would be the easiest to deal with.

Uh, *not.*

A slow grin tilted the corners of the stranger's lips up and he leaned closer. As he did so, his dark, intense eyes caught and reflected a reddish glimmer from one of the stained-glass light fixtures overhead.

Devilish. Dangerous. *Off-limits.*

Or so she tried to tell herself. But she suspected it was no use. Unless the guy had a hideous voice, he was altogether perfect. And since conversation wasn't even on the top ten list of the things she'd been picturing doing with this man since the second she'd set eyes on him, she suspected it wouldn't matter if he sounded like Roger Rabbit on speed.

"I think that's her purse you're using to clean up the spilled beer," he said.

Velvet voice. Soft. Husky. As smooth and warm as their very best whiskey—the kind she kept hidden beneath the bar for special customers. She felt every word he spoke on each of the nerve endings in her body.

Doomed. The new, reformed Cat Sheehan was utterly doomed.

Then what he'd said sunk in and Cat looked down at her hand. "Oh, my God, I'm so sorry," she said when she spied what she'd been using as a rag.

It was a small, cloth handbag belonging to a customer seated at the bar. Fortunately, the woman was one of their regulars, a bank teller named Julie. Even more fortunately, Julie was just as drooly-faced over the stranger as Cat, because she seemed to understand Cat's lapse into hot-man-induced dementia.

"It'll wash," Julie mumbled.

The man plucked the damp purse from Cat's limp fingers and handed it to its owner, giving her an intimate smile. "Maybe a drink on the house would help?"

Julie nodded dumbly. Cat was tempted to grab the woman's left hand and flip it over to remind her of the big diamond ring she'd been flashing in here since her engagement to some salesman. But she couldn't blame her.

Engaged or not, any woman would look twice...or dozens of times...at a man like this one.

Then he turned his attention back to Cat. His full, unwavering attention. "Hi. I'm your entertainment," he finally said, his voice low and intimate though she'd swear laughter danced behind his eyes.

"You're *very* good," she replied matter-of-factly.

A dimple flashed in one of his lean cheeks. "You haven't seen what I can do yet."

"Wild guess," she mumbled, her mind filling with possibilities of just what he *could* do. She had to give herself credit—only half were X-rated. Well, maybe sixty percent.

"You won't have to wait for long to find out," he said, his tone as suggestive as her words had been.

Oh, boy, did that set her heart flip-flopping in her chest.

Her expression must have given away her thoughts. His brown eyes darkened to near black and he leaned closer, both elbows now resting on the bar. "You sure you're gonna be able to handle it?"

She raised a challenging brow. "You think you're that good? That you can't be *handled*?"

"I've been known to shake the walls when I get going."

Cat grabbed the edge of the bar to steady herself and took a deep breath. She should walk away, ignore the comment, pretend she'd misunderstood.

She did none of the above. Instead, even though she knew she shouldn't step farther into the fire, she threw a spark right back at the solid stick of dynamite watching her with promise in his eyes. "I've been known to rattle a few walls myself."

His cocky grin faded and his jaw tightened a bit. *Tie game.* She'd definitely gotten under his skin, just as he had hers. Then he managed, "So you *play*, too?"

"Not lately," she admitted.

Nope, she hadn't *played* with a man in a very long time. Not since last year, when she'd briefly dated a rodeo cowboy, whose lack of finesse in the saddle had been equaled only by his lack of staying power.

He'd lasted about three-and-a-half minutes. *They'd* lasted about three-and-a-half dates.

"What instrument?" he asked.

The words, "a thick, eight-inch one is my preference," came to mind, but she bit back the reply. This game had gotten a bit *too* reckless for a woman who'd sworn off guys with trouble written all over them. This one was the absolute Yellow Pages of trouble. "Um…"

"I somehow see you as a sax woman."

Her mouth dropped open. She was definitely a sex woman, which she was being reminded of with every passing second. But, lord, he'd skipped right past the subtle innuendo, hadn't he?

"Or maybe clarinet?"

Her brow shot up. "You mean we were talking about *musical* instruments?"

"Of course." He managed to pull off a look of such complete innocence that Cat began to believe she really had misread their conversation. "What else would we have been talking about?"

Feeling heat rise in her face, she opened her mouth, then closed it, wondering how to gracefully back out of this enormous foot-in-mouth moment. She was about to tell him she was a virtuoso on the kazoo when she saw his shoulders shaking with suppressed amusement.

"Dog," she muttered, laughing even as she shook her head in admiration of how well he'd played her.

"Cat," he replied.

"Yes. Cat Sheehan."

He nodded. "I know."

Interesting. He knew who she was. Which left her at a disadvantage. "And you are…?"

He paused, a frown pulling at his brow so briefly she almost missed it. Then he admitted, "Call me Spence."

She'd rather call him guy-destined-to-be-naked-in-her-bed-by-midnight.

Not happening, she reminded herself. *This is supposed to be the new you.*

The new her might be trying to call the shots in the brain. But the old Cat—the hungry one whose entire body was sparking in reaction to this stranger named Spence—had control of everything from the neck down. Especially the, uh, *softest* parts.

Still, even the old, reckless Cat had never done the one-night stand thing. Despite what her sister might imagine, Cat wasn't *that* danger-loving. With a man like this one, however, she was beginning to understand the illicit allure of a bar hookup.

"Hi, Spence. Welcome to Temptation," she finally said.

"I like that."

"What?"

"Temptation."

Ooooh…definitely her kinda guy.

"I also liked the sign over your front door."

She instantly knew which one he meant—the hand-painted sign inviting those outside to *Enter Into Temptation.* She'd thought up the logo three years ago when she and Laine had taken over the bar from their mother, changing the name from Sheehan's Pub to Temptation. "Thanks. Seemed appropriate."

"I just didn't realize it was going to be quite so prophetic," he added, his tone husky.

She got his meaning instantly. He was every bit as tempted as she was. A long, shuddery breath escaped her lips. Unable to do much more than breathe and stand still, she stared at him. Right into those fathomless eyes.

He stared right back, just as intently, neither of them laughing or flirting any longer. They said nothing, yet exchanged a wealth of information. In twenty seconds they covered the basics—yes, they were both interested, and, yes, they were both aware of each other's interest. But it went deeper...they each knew that they could play games or do away with them right now. Because the palpable attraction made something happening between them inevitable.

They all but named the time and place.

Then his lips—God, those lips—parted, and he drew in a long, slow breath of air. His lids lowered slightly, half closing over his eyes, drawing her attention to his long, spiky black lashes. Visceral pleasure accompanied his inhalation, and she realized what he was doing.

Smelling her perfume. Inhaling it. Savoring it. Gaining sensual pleasure from the aroma of her skin.

Dangerous. Oh, he was dangerous. Because he was so damned appealing. A man who appreciated a woman's scent would appreciate so many other delightful things, wouldn't he? Tastes, touches, sensations.

Her pulse raced as the thick, heady silence dragged on, in spite of the cacophony all around them. At some point, she noted Julie pushing away and getting off her stool, until Cat and Spence were the only two people in this small corner of the bar.

Surrounded by others, but completely alone.

Cat hesitated as a sensation of déjà vu washed over her. How many times had she stood in this room, filled with chattering people—customers, family, friends—and felt that *exact* sensation of being alone, separated? It felt as if the world was moving all around her but she was frozen for one moment in time, looking at her life and wondering if she really was traveling the same path as everyone else. Because she so rarely felt in step with anyone.

Only now, in this timeless instant when she wondered just where she belonged and where she was going, she wasn't completely by herself. This dark-haired stranger was right there with her.

"Cat?" he asked, obviously sensing her confusion.

She blinked rapidly and shook her head, shaking off not only the strange sensation, but also the intensity of the moment. Forcing herself to focus, she shifted her gaze away, toward a customer who'd just taken a seat at the far end of the bar. She stepped over to him, trying to convince herself she had to get back to work when, in truth, she needed a chance to regain her sanity.

"The usual?" she said to the guy in the brown sport coat, a Friday night regular who liked his women easy and his martinis dirty.

He nodded. "If you can…spare the time," he said with a truly amused grin, probably having heard the quiver in her voice.

Behind her, she heard a long, low chuckle. As throaty and sensuous as every word Spence had spoken.

She deserved the reaction. She'd looked away first, losing their silent game of chicken, shocking even herself. Cat didn't remember the last time that had happened to her.

Being disconcerted around a man was something she had seldom experienced. Cat Sheehan had been able to hold her own with men since the tenth grade when she'd started busing tables at the family bar. She'd sassed the old-timers, ducked away from grabby strangers and eventually chosen her first lover from among the Saturday night regulars.

Never before had a man taken the upper hand from her—unless she'd wanted him to. This guy with his jet-black hair and his badass grin and his big, hard guitar had done it with a stare.

Which was why, after she'd served Mr. Sport Coat his martini, she was having such a hard time thinking of a single thing to say to the still-staring musician. How could she even try to explain away that silence as something other than what they both knew damn well it had been?

An invitation. A challenge. A promise. None of which she had any business accepting.

But oh, how tempting it was to consider it.

Good Lord, no wonder she was having a hard time coming up with any kind of response—much less a sassy comeback. Cat felt completely at a loss for words. Continuing the flirtation would be reinforcing her implied acceptance of every wicked thing he'd suggested with his eyes.

Ending it might just kill her.

He finally spared her by steering the conversation into neutral territory. "I do have the right place, don't I? You're expecting the Four G's?"

The Four G's…she instantly remembered the band from Tremont—the next town over—which she'd hired for this weekend's live entertainment. *Of course he's with the band, idiot. Isn't he carrying a guitar case?* She cleared her throat and nodded. "Uh, yes, definitely the right place. I'm… we're…glad to have you here."

Oh, yeah, she'd be glad to have him all right. Upstairs in her apartment. On the swing in the back garden.

Hell, on top of the bar might be nice.

Cat thrust the mental picture out of her head, promising herself she'd lay off the romance novels. And the occasional late-night blue movies on cable. And the erotic fantasies during her middle-of-the-night bubble baths. Because she had obviously become a sex-starved maniac.

She did have to give herself a little bit of a break. After all, it'd been a year since she'd had even bad sex. As for good sex? Whew, she wasn't sure she could remember when that had last happened. Which had to explain why she wanted this guy like a woman on the South Beach Diet wanted a baked potato. With fries on the side.

"Thanks. We were glad to get the call." Spence smiled, a cocky half smile that said he knew what she'd been doing—trying to act nonchalant and not quite succeeding. "Though it looks like a small audience."

"What, are you kidding?" she asked, glancing around the room, where at least twenty people sat at the usually empty tables. "This is a crowd for us, lately. As close to wall-to-wall as we've seen since they tore up the nearest intersection, banned on-street parking, and set up a horrendous detour."

Obviously hearing her disgust, he said, "You sound like you definitely need some entertainment this weekend."

Oh, he had no idea how much she needed entertainment. Or maybe he did. His tiny grin told her they were flirting again. This time—maybe because he'd let her regain her equilibrium with small talk about the bar—Cat felt more able to handle it. "I'm a little particular in how I get my…entertainment."

"Oh? Anything you'd care to share?"

Licking her lips, she did a classic blond hair toss—which she'd learned around the age of three—and reached for a martini shaker. She splashed a generous amount of vodka into it, dirtied it up with a splash of olive juice, then poured it for the guy at the end of the bar, knowing by the look in his eye that he was ready for another.

"I don't think so," she said when she returned her attention to Spence.

He shook his head. "Too bad. So I guess I'll just have to do my stuff for everyone else in the room."

"I somehow suspect the women in this place are going to like seeing you do your stuff," she replied, her tone dry.

"I somehow suspect I won't care what any *other* woman thinks."

Cat nibbled her bottom lip, seeing an expression that somehow resembled tenderness cross his face. As if he were no longer flirting, but being entirely serious. Which was ridiculous, considering they'd known each other all of a half hour.

She shook off the feeling. "They'll be a good audience, since you're here at their request. I asked the loyal regulars who've been sticking it out through the road construction to vote on what they wanted for the last few weekends we're open. Two of the three are strictly country and western, but this weekend Temptation is all about rock and roll, and you guys came highly recommended."

"Lucky me." Straightening, he lifted his guitar case off the floor and looked toward the door, where another guitar-carrying musician was entering. "Guess I'd better go."

He was going to be across the room, but for some silly reason she almost missed him. Maybe it was because she knew in a few minutes he would be the property of every on-the-make woman in the place. "Want me to send over a drink to keep your pipes wet?"

He nodded. "Just water, if you don't mind."

He started to walk away, then paused and looked back. Nodding toward something on the wall behind her, he lowered his voice and said, "By the way…*not me*. And hopefully not *you*."

She was still puzzling over the remark after he'd reached the stage. Then, finally, she realized what he'd been talking about. Swiveling on her heel, she looked up at the sign above the bar. It had been hand-painted by the same artist who'd done the one out front, as well as the murals in the back hallway.

Though Spence's answer had brought up a number of complications, the sign posed a simple question.

Who can resist Temptation?

DYLAN SPENCER HAD FALLEN madly in love twice in his life.

The first time had been at age seven when he'd been introduced to his ultimate destiny: the greatest form of music ever created. He'd been visiting his grandparents' house in New England for the holidays and one of his older cousins had gotten a Van Halen album for Christmas. It had been love at first riff.

The year had been 1985 and the record had been 1984 and Dylan had decided then and there that bass player Michael Anthony had been touched by God.

● Dylan had been completely enthralled. His parents—who never listened to anything that didn't feature fat Italian opera singers—had not been. Particularly when they'd caught Dylan entertaining all the neighborhood kids with a rousing, nearly R-rated rendition of "Hot For Teacher."

Thinking they could steer his love for music, and encourage his rather amazing natural musical abilities, they'd signed him up for piano lessons.

He'd been kicked out when he'd broken into Queen's "Bohemian Rhapsody" during an end-of-the-year recital.

By ten he was air guitaring his way through life. By

twelve, after five years of relentless begging, he had his own real bass guitar and it had been practically glued to his hands ever since.

Yeah. Rock and roll had been his first experience with instant obsession.

Cat Sheehan had been his second.

Throughout the evening, while he stayed perfectly in sync with his bandmates, putting his all into the music, he kept at least part of his attention on her. The woman who'd taken his breath away from the moment he'd first laid eyes on her.

Cat wasn't hard to keep track of—she definitely stood out. From here, behind the glare of the small spotlights, her long golden hair looked almost silver. Occasionally, she'd smooth it back off her cheek with one graceful lift of her finger, so that it framed her perfect face.

He wasn't close enough to focus on the deep, ocean-green of her eyes. But he definitely watched the graceful movements of her slim body, clad in tight-as-sin jeans and a sleeveless white tank top. Also tight. Also sinful.

Working the bar as if she'd been born behind it, Cat didn't even have to look at the labels of the bottles from which she poured. Her hand never faltered as she made any drink ordered. She moved with a dancer's grace, able to pull a draft of beer off the tap, circle around and set it down in front of a customer in one long, fluid movement a ballerina would envy.

Chatting easily with everyone, she smiled often—that dazzling smile taking his breath away from all the way across the room. At one point, he even thought he heard her throaty laugh over all the other noise in the place. The sound was distinct because of the reaction it caused in him—instant awareness. Instant hunger. Instant heat.

She affected him like the music affected him.

Deeply. Intimately. Physically.

But it wasn't just that. He liked hearing the laugh and seeing the smile because they countered the weariness in her brow and the slight slump of her shoulders, which he'd noticed as soon as they'd started talking earlier. He didn't know what was troubling Cat. But he planned to find out.

"This place is wild," Josh Garrity yelled from the other side of the small stage. The crowd was roaring its approval at the end of their second set. If the walls weren't still shaking from the Aerosmith song they'd just finished, they were from the applause. "You think they'll let us take a real break this time, Spence?"

Dylan nodded as he carefully put his beloved Fender back into its case and turned off his Voodoo amp. Josh played guitar and sang lead most of the time; Dylan was on bass, doing some of the vocalizations, as well. But it seemed as if all the songs the crowd had been yelling for were Dylan's and his throat was now almost raw. "If they don't, neither one of us is going to have any voice left at all."

Nodding, Josh waved at the audience, which had swelled in size over the past few hours until every table was taken. "Stay, drink, be patient. We'll be back in twenty," he shouted into the microphone, trying to be heard over the applause and whistles.

The audience cheered a bit more, but since the band members were already putting their instruments down, they gradually quieted. The typical mad race for the restrooms and fresh rounds quickly got underway. As did the pickup conversations going on between the hopeful single guys and their prospects.

"The *place* isn't the only thing that's wild," their drummer Jeremy said as he lowered his drumsticks and rose from his stool. "The brunette in the jean miniskirt who was sitting at the table closest to the stage wasn't wearing any underwear." He shook his head. "It was like she *wanted* me to see…everything."

Seeing the shock on Jeremy's face, Dylan hid a jaded grin. Jeremy, Josh's younger brother, was their newest member, a baby-faced nineteen-year-old. Jeremy hadn't yet realized that rock-and-roll groupies didn't always limit their adulation to the famous groups who were household names. Sometimes local bands—like theirs—had their own fan bases. The familiar faces in tonight's crowd certainly bore that out.

That was one of the drawbacks to the business, as far as Dylan was concerned. He played for his own pleasure, his own release. He had never been interested in the fans or the lifestyle or any of the garbage that went along with it. He just liked to head-bang on occasion. Which was probably why he'd never gone any further with his music than to small places like this, in small Texas towns.

"So, you gonna go over and talk to her or just keep staring at her like some lovesick mutt?"

Dylan jerked his attention toward Billy Banks, the final member of their four-man group, who wailed like a madman on the keyboard. Banks was grinning that sardonic grin of his, brown eyes sparkling behind the wire-framed glasses he wore to give himself the appearance of an intellectual rock and roller. He liked to think of himself as the Lennon of their group.

The women seemed to like it, too. Between Banks's brainy persona and deep-rooted mischievous streak, Jeremy's fresh-faced innocence, Josh's breezy surfer style and Dylan's own long-haired rebel thing, they had a regular stream of females ready to keep them company whenever they desired it.

Dylan hadn't desired it. Not in a long time.

But Banks sure had, which wasn't surprising. Ever since they'd met at freshman orientation in college, where they'd been the two youngest people in the room, Billy Banks had proved himself to be two things: woman-crazy and the best, most loyal friend Dylan had ever had.

"Well? You going over? You've been eyeing her all night."

"You're seeing things," Dylan mumbled, choosing to pretend he didn't know what the guy was talking about.

"Oh, come on, man, I thought you were gonna short out the sound system because the mike was getting so wet with your drool every time you looked at that blond bartender."

"Bite me."

Banks smirked. "You oughtta save that line for her."

Shooting Banks—who was as close to him as a brother—a look that threatened bodily injury, Dylan walked to the rear of the stage to amp everything down.

Banks soon crouched beside him to help. "She is totally hot," he said, sounding contrite. Definitely out of character for Banks, who never regretted anything he did.

Dylan hesitated for one second, wondering how much to reveal. Finally, between clenched teeth, he admitted the truth. "She's Cat Sheehan."

Banks jerked so hard he almost fell on his ass. His eyes widened and his jaw dropped. When Dylan confirmed the truth of his words with a nod, Banks emitted a long, low whistle. "*The* Cat woman herself, huh?"

Dylan nodded again, knowing he didn't have to say anything more. Banks knew all about Cat. He was probably the only one who knew the entire truth about Dylan's relationship with the blonde.

The one-sided relationship that had been going on for several years now.

"Did you know she'd be here?"

He shook his head. "I recognized the building when I pulled up outside. Her family used to own the place. But the name's changed. I figured she was long gone."

Banks nodded. "Did she know who you were?"

No. She hadn't. Which still slightly burned him. But he didn't want Banks to know that. So he shrugged in disinterest. "We've barely spoken."

Banks merely smirked, the sorry son of a bitch, knowing Dylan much too well to be fooled by that. Then he looked over Dylan's shoulder, toward the other side of the bar, nodding as he sought out Cat. "So you finally have your shot," he murmured. "Your dream girl has been looking at you all night like she needs a sugar fix and you're a giant Tootsie Roll."

Banks's words brought some intense images to mind and he had to busy his hands winding cable to keep them from shaking. "You're imagining things," he said. "She's barely paid attention to us at all."

Banks let out a bark of laughter that caused several people standing nearby to glance over in curiosity. "Man, you are losing it if you didn't see the way that girl kept her eyes glued to you. Except every time you looked in her direction—then she turned away right quick."

Okay, it was possible. He and Cat had shared a sexy, flirtatious conversation before the rest of the band had shown up. There had been some definite spark, a genuine intensity between them.

A lazy smile widened his lips at the memory. He had never fallen into such instant sync with anyone before. And he'd certainly never been so completely affected by a woman before—at least, not in his adult life. Even now, nearly two hours later, he could still smell the warm, sultry aroma of her perfume and hear her throaty laugh.

"She's yours for the taking," Banks added. "You can finally have what you always wanted."

Dylan was shaking his head even before Banks finished his ridiculous statement. His friend was wrong. Very, very wrong.

Cat might be interested now. Judging by the heat-filled moments they'd shared earlier, he'd say she probably was.

Didn't matter. Because the minute she found out his true identity, the spark would fade, the intensity would disappear and his chances along with it. He knew it. Knew it like he knew his own guitar.

She was interested in Spence, the bass-playing rock and roller with a strut and a sneer and a cocky-as-hell attitude. Which was pretty funny, come to think of it, in a you-poor-sorry-sucker way. Because the man she was attracted to didn't exist. He was a phantom. A facade. A fictional character.

In truth, Dylan Spencer was a complete and utter fraud.

2

If TEMPTATION HAD HAD more nights like this, they might have had enough money to hire a better attorney for their fight to stay open. Cat couldn't get over the people who'd squeezed in over the past couple of hours, all of them thirsty. And hungry, judging by the way Zeke, their cook, was whipping out everything on their limited menu just as fast as he could.

The Four G's, music seemed to have had some kind of Pied Piper effect on the residents of Kendall, many of whom were former patrons who hadn't wanted to deal with the hassles of road construction in recent months. Temptation hadn't been this crowded since the spring, when an erroneous rumor had circulated that they were hosting a wet T-shirt contest.

If it would have saved the bar, Cat would have given it some serious consideration.

"I think I'm going to have to kill Tess when and if she ever comes back."

Cat quickly swung two beers, a Sex on the Beach, and a mojito onto a serving tray and gave Dinah, their part-time waitress, a commiserating smile. "I don't think any of us ever expected to have nights like these during the last few weeks we're open. I'm sure Tess and Laine would both have stuck around if they'd thought we were going to actually be having *crowds*, rather than our usual *quartets*."

Cat firmly believed that. She was still a bit upset with Laine for taking off on some daring, photographic wild-fire adventure in California. Secretly, however, she had to concede she was glad Laine was there to help their Aunt Jen, whose house was being threatened by the fires engulfing the state. Besides, Laine had been talking for a long time about how much she wanted one of her photos on the cover of the magazine she worked for, *Century*. This might actually be her shot. So while she was peeved at her, Cat couldn't be too upset.

As for Tess, their other waitress…well, with her, you never knew what to expect. Like the way she'd stumbled into the job at Temptation a few years back. She'd started waitressing to work off a bar tab she couldn't pay and had never left.

Unpredictable. That described Tess. So her deciding to take off last Tuesday night to help distribute some old guy's money was entirely understandable. Unlike Laine, at least Tess had asked Cat first if she minded, and had even offered her some of her newfound riches.

Cat hadn't accepted the money—it was too late for that. But she *had* minded her friend leaving. Not so much because she needed Tess's help—or Laine's, for that matter—but because she'd had this whole sappy image of the four of them crying in each other's arms during the last few weeks the bar was open.

She hadn't told Tess or Laine that. In fact, she'd urged Tess to go. And Laine…well, after their argument, she hadn't been surprised her sister had taken off.

She'd missed them both ever since, much more than she'd ever have expected. Which was silly, really, since she'd always known everybody was destined to leave. Her grandparents, her father. Her remarried mother. Her brilliant sister.

Cat ending up alone had been inevitable. But she'd always thought she'd at least have Temptation.

Dinah clucked her tongue and shook her head, making her poufed platinum blond hair teeter a bit to one side. "I still can't get over the two of them bailing out of here. You sure you don't want me to tell your mama…"

"Don't even think about it," Cat said, already grabbing two bottles of Bud for the guys waving to her from the end of the bar. "She's upset enough about the pub closing. The last thing I need is to have her come down here to help out, because you know her helping out would mean me losing my mind."

Dinah, who'd been one of her mother's closest friends since their high school years, chuckled. "It's just because she worries."

"She worries, I snap. Without Laine here to referee, it'd be a nightmare."

"You think it'll be like this all weekend?" Dinah asked. "Because if so, we might need to call in some backup. Tess did say she was going to be as close as Austin…"

Cat shook her head. "It's okay, I already took care of it. I called an old friend and tapped her to help out tomorrow night."

Dinah, a fifty-something native Texan whose heart was bigger than most people's minivans, sighed in visible relief. "Thank the Lord. I don't think my knees could take another night like this one."

Cat purposely looked at the beer mug she was holding under the tap and kept her voice casual as she asked, "How are *Zeke's* knees holding up?"

Silence. Then Dinah squawked, "You bad girl...as if I know. The man's more skittish than a virgin in a frathouse."

Knowing Dinah had had her eye on Zeke for about two years, ever since Laine and Cat had hired the man to cook for their pub clientele, Cat frowned. "You're running out of time, you know. If you're going to make something happen, you'd better do it while you two are still working together every day."

Dinah rolled her eyes. "Sugar, I could bathe naked in that man's deep fryer and he wouldn't look."

"I dunno...warm oil, a hot kitchen, spicy smells. Sounds pretty sexy to me."

"Me, too," a male voice said. The hair standing on end all over her body told her exactly which male voice.

Crud. She'd gotten so distracted chatting with Dinah about the older woman's romantic possibilities that she'd completely forgotten about her own.

No. He's not a possibility.

She'd been telling herself that for two hours, every throaty, wickedly sexy song the band performed reminding her of just how dangerous getting involved with Spence would be. Even if he had made her almost melt into a puddle when he'd sung one song she hadn't recognized, about making love in the moonlight on a windswept beach to a woman with fire in her eyes. Made her want to take a drive down to the Galveston coast. With him.

But no. It'd never happen. He was a long-haired musician playing tiny bars in Nowhereville, Texas, for heaven's sake. The man probably didn't even *own* a car. Spence was definitely not the steady, reliable type she'd been telling herself she needed to find. Far, far from it!

The flirting was over with. The guy was a hunk and a

half, but so were a lot of other guys. And all of them were the type who walked away.

She'd had enough of those, dammit. From here on out, she was going to be strictly business with this particular one. So she offered him an impersonal smile. "Hey, I was afraid the crowd was never going to let you guys take a break."

"Me, too," he said.

Without being asked, she opened a bottle of icy cold water and slid it to him. He picked it up, giving her a grateful nod, and lifted it to his lips.

Lips. Don't think of the lips. You never notice the lips of the guy at the bank or the post office.

She looked down, her gaze falling on his throat. Her breaths deepened as she watched the way his pulse pounded in his neck and the muscles leading to his shoulders rippled with his every movement. All glisteny with a sheen of sweat. Probably tasted salty.

She added more no-no words to her list. *Neck. Shoulders. Muscles. Glisteny. Salty.*

"Thanks," he said as he lowered the nearly empty bottle. "Those lights are pretty hot. I was half wishing I'd worn less clothes." He cleared his throat. "I mean, lighter clothes. Shorts or something."

Less clothes? No pants? She might as well just give this up right now. Because no matter how hard she tried to keep her mind focused and professional, she kept sliding down this slippery slope of attraction to this man. She couldn't possibly survive another round of sexual roulette with him.

But at least this time, Spence was looking uncomfortable, as well. Funny, the way he'd stammered over the words he'd said, about wearing less clothes. As if he, too, had recognized the naughty implication and had been slightly embarrassed about it.

It was cute, that sheepish look on his face. Not to mention completely unexpected. Embarrassment and this guy went together about as naturally as pork chops and a vegetarian.

"It is awfully hot in here, don't you think?" he finally said, filling the thick silence. How bizarre, this feeling of being in a silent bubble, when all around them voices chattered and glasses tinkled. But, like before, all of that seemed very far away.

"Yeah, well, uh...I guess the crowd of naked bodies makes it feel even hotter," Cat said.

Then she bit her tongue. *Bodies.* Another definite no-no word when Spence was around. If this kept up, she was going to have the vocabulary of a ten-month-old.

"Uh, Cat, did you say what I think you said?"

Sure, she'd said the crowd of bodies...oh, God, she hadn't said *naked*, had she? *Tell me I didn't say naked.*

"Because we're pretty open to playing at unusual venues, but an entirely naked audience, well, that could get a little...sticky." His lips twitched, and she knew he was trying to hold back his laughter.

Cat blushed. Literally felt hot blood rise in her face and flood her cheeks. No guy had *ever* made her blush.

"Slip of the tongue," she muttered, grabbing for any halfway believable excuse she could find. "I mean, you know, the words, they sort of go together. Naked. And bodies. I might just as easily have said *dead* and bodies."

Argh! Just stick a spike through your hand and get it over with, Cat. It'd be less painful than this.

"I think I'd prefer naked ones to dead ones," he murmured.

She kept prattling on, like an out of control car careening toward a cliff. "You know what I mean, though, right? Some words are kind of a natural fit. Like fried and oysters."

His lips twitched again. "Most people would say fried goes better with chicken...but if you prefer *oysters*..."

"I don't. Prefer oysters, I mean, no matter what their, uh, reputation," she said, wondering why she'd had to immediately latch on the sex food group when there were so many others available. Bacon and eggs. Hot and tamale.

Dead and duck.

"Me, neither. Nasty little things," he said, obviously still talking about the oysters.

Cat nodded in agreement. "Shiny and slippery and wet."

One of his brows shot up. "Shiny...slippery...wet?"

Cat pictured putting her mouth in front of a firing squad for continuing to bring both their minds to places they had no business being. She closed her eyes, unable to manage a single word. She could only shake her head in dismay. When, in the name of heaven, had Cat Sheehan turned into a babbling idiot?

Spence started to laugh—a low, husky laugh that made her tingle, all over. "I'd offer you a shovel, but I don't have one on me. Besides, you're doing a pretty good job digging yourself deeper into this hole all on your own."

"If you'll excuse me, I think I'll go shoot myself now."

"I just told you I don't have a shovel, Cat."

"So you can't bury me?"

"Uh huh."

She tapped the tip of her index finger on her cheek, thinking about it, even as she gave in and laughed a little with him. "Hmm, so how about backing up ten minutes and starting this whole thing over?"

Spence leaned over the bar, propping his chin on his fist. "Hi. Thanks for the water. What'd you think of the music?"

"You guys really are good," she said, thrilled at the chance to keep the conversation neutral.

"Thanks." He leaned closer, raising his voice as more people crowded close to the bar, waving at Cat to place their orders. "We have a lot of fun doing it."

Getting back to work, she filled a few mugs, poured a few shots, blew off a few jerks, then returned her attention to the bass player in the corner. "I really liked that song you did about the girl with the fire in her eyes and the moonlight on her hair. Who sang it originally? I didn't recognize it."

Spence shrugged, lifted his bottle to his mouth and sipped more water. After sipping, he lowered the bottle and wiped the moisture off his lips with the back of his hand.

Cat just stared, acknowledging the truth: the man was poetry in motion. No small talk in the world was going to make her oblivious to that.

"You didn't recognize it because I wrote it," he said.

Wrote it. Wrote poetry? She blinked a couple of times, trying to backtrack and remember what the heck they'd been talking about before he'd gotten her all distracted with his water-drinking abilities. Then she remembered. "You wrote *that* song? The one about the hot night and the whispers in the dark?"

Wow. She never would have guessed. Not only because the music had been so good, but also because of the unbridled emotion of the words, juxtaposed against the raw, haunting power of the melody. It had sounded…hungry. That was the only word she could find to describe it. "I'm impressed. You must have had quite a lot of inspiration to write such a powerful song."

She hadn't been fishing for information. She *hadn't*. It was none of her business what inspired him to write such a sensual, heated ballad. But she still held her breath, waiting for his response, hoping he wouldn't say he'd written it for the love of his life. His longtime girlfriend.

God, please, not his wife!

When his answer came, she couldn't help feeling a sharp stab of disappointment. Because a faraway look of longing and hunger accompanied his words. "I wrote it for a girl I was crazy about a long, long time ago."

HE'D WRITTEN the song for *her*.

Staring at Cat, Dylan focused on those vivid green eyes of hers—those catlike green eyes. He silently willed her to read the truth that screamed loudly in his brain but didn't cross his lips. *It was you. It was always you.*

The girl in the song, with moonlight shining on her hair, had been Cat Sheehan bathed in the glow of an enormous bonfire the night of a homecoming game many years ago. If he closed his eyes, he could still see her there, standing completely alone, staring at the flames. She'd been lost in thought, seeming separate and distinct from the rowdy teenagers all around her.

It was so easy even now to remember the way her eyes had glittered and her skin had taken on the golden sheen of the fire. Her hair had positively come alive, as brilliant and dazzling as the flames that leaped and crackled against the star-filled night sky. And even from several feet away, he'd seen the way her lips had moved, as if she were whispering something for her ears alone.

He'd wanted to be the one she whispered to.

Wondering why she looked so sad, so serious and so lonely, he'd even moved closer. He'd been driven to understand why she stood there by herself, as if a curtain had descended between her and everyone else. Everyone except him.

Then someone had taken her arm and she'd rejoined the living, laughter on her lips, as always.

And, as always, she hadn't even noticed him standing there in the shadows. Apparently, she'd *never* really noticed him. Certainly not enough to make an impression. Because judging by tonight, Cat had absolutely no idea that they'd been classmates at Kendall High a mere nine years ago.

It wasn't her fault. Cat had never shunned him; he'd just been too intimidated to *make* her notice him. Not intimidated by her...but by the intensity of his own feelings, which had simply overwhelmed him, particularly after the night of the bonfire.

Because that had been the night he'd realized there was so much more depth to the beautiful, vivacious Cat than she ever let the world see. The night he'd realized the two of them had something very deep and intrinsic in common.

Their solitude.

Things had changed, though. Because now, she definitely noticed him. For the past ten minutes, during her adorable, fumbling conversation—which was so unlike the self-assured Cat he remembered—she'd been staring at him with intensity, interest and pure, physical want.

He knew the look. Tonight, he almost certainly mirrored it.

Then again, if she'd ever really looked at him, she would have seen that look on his face throughout the entire year they'd gone to school together.

Not meeting his eyes as she rubbed the surface of the bar with a damp rag, Cat said, "You have a lot of talent."

"Thanks. Music's my passion."

"Your *only* passion?"

"Not only. There's also video games."

One of her delicate brows lifted. "Rock and roll and video games. So are you just a mature-looking fifteen-year-old?"

"Smart-ass." He didn't elaborate on the video game thing, thinking she probably wasn't ready to hear that he didn't merely *play* them. He created and developed them. Very successfully.

"Goes with the territory," she said with a shrug.

"Being a smart-ass?"

She looked past him, nodded at someone, then got busy making a couple of scotch and sodas. "Yeah. Can't take things too seriously when perfect strangers are talking to you like they're your best friend night after night. Telling you their troubles. It'd be too damned depressing, especially for someone like me."

He hadn't thought of it that way. Then, curious, he asked, "Someone like you?"

Cat shrugged, suddenly looking uncomfortable. "I mean, well, anyone who gets riled up a bit too easily, like I used to do."

Riled up easily? Oh, yeah, Cat Sheehan had had a reputation for that. He didn't know if the Kendall High football team had ever gotten over being told they were a bunch of spiteful, fatheaded kindergartners with big egos and little dicks.

She'd done it during a pep rally.

Over a loudspeaker.

In front of the whole school.

Cat had gotten suspended. She'd also earned the never-ending devotion of all the freshmen who'd been used as walking punching bags by some of the bullying members of the football team.

"So you still get riled up too easily?" he asked.

She shook her head. "Not me. Miss Reasonable, Miss

Calm, Cool and Collected, that's me these days. I can handle anything."

She tried to meet his eye, tried to maintain a sincere expression, but didn't quite manage it. Dylan couldn't help it. He started to laugh.

She shot him a dirty look, then dissolved into helpless laughter, too. "Okay, so maybe you are getting to know me. And the answer is yes, I probably do take things too personally and get myself in trouble on occasion. But I have handled things pretty well all on my own for a long time now. Despite what anyone in my family might say. And I'm determined to stay out of trouble, in spite of some of the things I'd really like to do."

He wanted to ask if she'd told off any dumb jocks lately but didn't want to tip his hand too soon. "For instance?"

Her smile faded, that tension returning to her slim body. "I fantasize about driving one of those bulldozers outside right onto the lawn of the courthouse and leaving a big Porta-John on the front steps. It'd have a big Welcome Home sign for the city officials who voted me out of business."

Cat's words gave him the opening he'd been waiting for…a chance to try to find out why she appeared so tense. "So, are you really closing the bar?"

Her mouth tightened. "End of the month. Demolition ball swings in July. Gotta make way for progress…how could we ever live without four lanes?"

"That blows."

She nodded, blinking rapidly, and Dylan recognized her anguish. He now understood the slump in Cat's shoulders, the unhappiness that had likely caused those dark circles under her beautiful eyes.

Cat was hurting.

Sure, she was playing tough girl—hadn't she always?

But the pain beneath the surface would be obvious to a blind man.

"Is there anything I can do?" He figured there wasn't, but needed to ask, anyway.

"Just keep rocking the walls down this weekend so we can go out firmly in the black…and so I'll have a little money to live on while I figure out what I want to be when I grow up."

"I can't picture you being unsure of yourself for long, Cat Sheehan," he murmured, hearing the intensity in his voice.

She apparently heard it, too. Her eyes narrowed in skepticism. "You think you know me already, huh?"

Oh, yeah. He knew her. He'd known her for years. He'd watched her with simple devotion when he'd been a young, geeky kid to whom she'd never have given a second look. And he'd seen her in his dreams in the years that had followed.

"Yeah. I think I do know you."

But not as well as he planned to.

LATE THAT NIGHT, as Dylan helped the rest of the guys load their equipment and instruments into Josh's van, he tried to ignore Banks's curious stares. Banks had been watching him, a knowing grin on his face, every time Dylan had wandered over to the bar to talk to Cat when they were on break. During their final set, he'd thought his friend was going to explode with curiosity. Only the fact that the crowd had been so responsive—not letting them wrap up the night until they'd played an hour longer than scheduled—had distracted the guy.

But now they were alone. Josh and Jeremy had gone back inside for the last of Jeremy's drums. Banks made full use of the opportunity. "So, what happened? You going back in there for a late-night *rendezvous*?"

"Big words, Banks. Still working on being the smart one?"

"I don't think anyone's going to figure out I've got a 130 IQ just because I know how to pronounce the word *rendezvous*."

"One-thirty, hmm? I'm so sorry."

It was an old bone of contention and a constant source of baiting. Because Dylan's was just a smidge higher.

His friend smirked. "Warning, warning, comparing IQs...your geek-o-meter is in the red zone."

"F. You." But Dylan was smiling as he said it. He finished storing the microphones and amps, then helped Banks load up his keyboard.

"So, seriously, man, what are you going to do about the Cat woman?"

"Don't call her that."

"Right, 'cause, uh, she was much younger when you went nuts over her? So, it's Cat girl, huh?"

"Do you ever shut up?"

"You roomed with me in college, so you already know the answer to that question. Now stop stalling. Did she recognize you? Did she realize you were the same nerdy little nobody who used to practically wet your Dockers whenever she came around back in high school?"

Banks. Couldn't live with him. Couldn't kill him and throw his body off the Chrysler Building.

"She didn't remember me."

Banks had the courtesy not to laugh. In fact, he frowned a bit. "Well, you can't be too surprised, can you? I found your high school yearbook one time in college. You look *nothing* like you did back then."

High school. Seemed like a lifetime ago.

He'd only attended public school for one year—his senior year—and he'd been only fifteen years old the day he'd started. A skinny kid who'd been accepted into a dozen colleges before he'd even started shaving.

He'd wanted to be normal. Just...normal. Instead of the whiz kid who'd skipped a few grades in the exclusive private schools his parents insisted he attend. His one outlet— which had driven his parents nuts—was his nonstop devotion to his music. Even though his mom and dad had ranted about how he was burning his brain cells, betraying his intelligence and making a mockery of his brilliant musical gifts, he'd never stopped working out his teen angst with his stereo or his guitar.

Until that year. When he'd finally gotten them to agree to let him finish out school with regular kids for a change, in a public high school.

Their agreement had come at a cost. A high one.

His music. For the entire school year.

That'd been the price—he could spend his senior year at Kendall High if he agreed to let his father lock away his guitar and his entire CD collection.

God, it'd been hard. Particularly when he'd started school and realized a fifteen-year-old senior wasn't going to fit in very well anywhere. He'd missed his music terribly. So badly he thought about giving up— about going back to his old school less than a week into the new year.

Then he'd seen her—Cat Sheehan, the high school sophomore who'd fired his imagination and awoken every angsty teenage hormone in his body. She'd been the most beautiful girl he'd ever seen and her smile had literally made the breath leave his lungs.

So he'd stuck it out, somehow making it work, if only so he could catch glimpses of her throughout the day. Could feel his heart skip a beat when she smiled that smile.

Could share, if only from a distance, in her delightfully wicked personality.

And after the night of the bonfire, he'd made it his personal mission to find out why there seemed to be another side to Cat that no one else in the world ever saw.

He never had. But maybe now, he'd have another chance.

Eventually, he'd found a way to fit in at Kendall High. He'd built his own group of friends. He'd done the brain thing—chess club, honor roll, debate team. He'd made his parents proud, devoting the entire year to more "appropriate" pursuits.

And he'd kept his promise, staying away from his guitar. But that hadn't stopped him from writing songs in his head. Songs about the blond angel who barely even knew he existed.

"I mean, it's not like you two had any classes together or anything, right?" Banks asked, still apparently thinking he needed to make Dylan feel better. "You were the same age, but you were a couple of years ahead of her."

"Right."

"So it's not like she knew you and then forgot about you."

"You don't have to try to cheer me up," Dylan said, surprised to realize it was the truth. "Like you said, I don't look anything like I did then."

Definitely not. Then he'd been a skinny runt, a geek and a freak. Nowhere near the realm of Cat Sheehan and her crowd.

Her crowd...well, actually, she hadn't had one. She'd fit in everywhere. Not a stuck-up cheerleader, not a druggie, not a jock, not a brain. She'd just been this nice, smart, funny girl who happened to look like a goddess. One who had a caustic wit and a strong sense of justice that could either get her out of trouble or—probably more often—deeper into it.

She'd been the girl everyone wanted to be like. The girl who'd told off the football squad. Who'd organized a blood drive when one of their classmates had been in a serious car accident. And who, on one occasion, had come to the vocal defense of a nerdy kid who'd made the enormous mistake of sitting at the jocks' table at lunchtime.

That'd been him.

She'd swooped in right before he'd gotten himself pounded. Taking him by the arm, she'd smiled brightly, saying, "You promised you'd sit with me, cutie." Then she'd pulled him up and tugged him away, the determination in her eye and the firm set of her lips daring anyone to try to stop her. Beelining to another corner of the cafeteria—a *safer* corner—she'd pushed him into a seat and plopped down next to him, staying for a good three minutes, to keep up appearances.

He hadn't been able to get a word out of his sawdust-dry mouth. But that'd been okay. She'd chatted nonstop about inane things—teachers, grades, the unfairness of the dress code.

Personally, Dylan had blessed the dress code. Because if her skirts had been any shorter, he'd have been unable to function at all in school.

Once the beefy crowd had left, she'd stood, saying, "Stay away from the fatheads, kid. Just remember, you'll be buying and selling them a hundred times over in ten years." Then, with a wink, she'd snagged his apple off his lunch tray and sauntered away. Leaving him sitting there, gaping, staring after her.

He'd loved her from that moment on, even knowing

he'd probably never see her again after he graduated from high school. And he hadn't.

Until tonight.

"So are you going back in there to make something happen?"

"Why the hell are you so interested in my love life?" Dylan asked with a frown. "Weren't there a half-dozen women slipping you their phone numbers tonight?"

Banks shrugged. "A dozen, at least." Then his eyes narrowed. "Which was nothing compared to the ones trying to slip *you* their phone numbers. By the way, thanks for the spillover."

Dylan just shrugged, saved from replying when Josh and Jeremy returned from inside. They quickly finished loading the gear, then closed up the van.

"See ya tomorrow night," Josh said as he got into the driver's seat.

Dylan nodded, then glanced at Jeremy, who was climbing onto the enormous motorcycle he'd bought a few months back. Since Dylan cringed every time he saw Jeremy on the thing, he could only imagine what his parents thought. "Don't kill yourself, kid," he called as the younger man rode away.

"Now, go back in there and make your move," Banks said as he unlocked his car."

Dylan shook his head. He wasn't ready yet. Wasn't ready to deal with the repercussions of what would happen when Cat found out the truth. "It's late. I'll talk to her tomorrow."

Face it, you want to enjoy it a little longer.

He did. He wanted just this weekend—tomorrow and Sunday night—of being the dark, dangerous stranger Cat Sheehan had been so attracted to. Then he'd tell her the truth. And go back to being the invisible guy.

But not now. Now it was time to go home and process everything.

Unfortunately, Banks, the bastard, had something else in mind. "By the way, Spence, are you missing something?"

Dylan raised a wary brow.

Banks's expression screamed mischief. Dylan had seen the look enough in college to know his friend was up to something. Something he wasn't going to like. Like the time he'd taken Dylan's clothes out of the bathroom while he was showering in their coed dorm, stranding him there.

Of course, Banks's plan had backfired. Wrapped in a towel and dripping with righteous anger—not to mention water—Dylan had gotten the attention of a *lot* of girls as he'd stalked down the hall toward his room. Including one Banks had been after throughout their junior year. Whenever his friend got too obnoxious, Dylan mentioned the name Karen Dennison and it shut him right up.

"What did you do?" he asked, not sure he wanted to know.

"You forgetting you need something to get in your car?"

Patting the pocket of his ratty jean jacket, which was slung over his arm, he winced when he did not hear a familiar jingle. No keys. "You sack of…"

"She'll be happy to let you in to look for them, I bet. She's just all alone in the dark," Banks said with a wave of his hand. Then he got into his own car, revved up the engine so he couldn't hear the names Dylan was calling him, and took off.

Leaving Dylan stranded, with no way home and no keys. Not unless he entered into Temptation and found them.

3

Exhausted and confused about the amazing man who'd walked into her life tonight, Cat was about to flip the lock on the front door when she saw a large form appear right outside. The unexpectedness of it brought a startled gasp to her lips—until she recognized the face.

"Spence?" she said, opening the door.

"I forgot something," he explained, looking uncomfortable.

Hmm...had he *really* forgotten something? Or was this a ruse to get her alone. More important—did she care?

Cat stepped back and ushered him in. "You just made it. Ten more minutes and I'd have been upstairs, sound asleep."

Looking curious, Spence stepped inside. "Upstairs?"

She shouldn't have given him that information. Shouldn't have let this gorgeous stranger—to whom she was altogether too attracted—know she lived right upstairs. Slept right upstairs. Had a big, comfortable bed, right upstairs.

She told herself all that, then nodded and spilled her guts, anyway. "Yes, I have an apartment right above Temptation. Live there all by my lonesome."

God, she might as well have invited him up, it probably would have sounded more honest and less pathetic.

"Convenient," was all he said as he stepped aside so she could push the door shut behind him.

The click of the door shut out the rest of the world, leaving them entirely alone. Completely, intoxicatingly alone.

The lights were all off in the main seating area of Temptation. One fixture, covered with smoked red glass, remained lit over the bar. It cast interesting pools of crimson throughout the room, its color whispering of sin and wickedness.

One additional dim light, which she usually left lit for security, provided a bit more illumination from the back hallway. Enough to reveal the skeletal legs of the chairs rising from the tables where Cat had put them up to sweep. But it wasn't strong enough to banish the shadows in the corners, on the stage or beside the jukebox. Nor to illuminate Spence's face well enough for her to gauge his mood. His intentions.

The pub at night was moody, secretive, sensuous… which matched *her* mood. The wood paneling caught bits of light, even as it creaked in late-night restlessness. Overhead, a fan spun lazily, its whir rustling the front blinds a bit. Their click was the only sound in an otherwise silent room.

That silence was thick, palpable, and Cat would bet Spence could hear the pounding of her heart if he listened for it.

All her internal alarms were ringing at the danger. Not that she feared physical danger from Spence. No, she simply feared she could very easily make a mistake she'd regret in the morning.

"Did you really forget something?" she finally asked, wondering if he heard the huskiness in her tone, the thickness caused by her suddenly dry mouth.

"Yeah."

She crossed her arms and tilted her head back in challenge. Leaning her hip against an empty table, she peered at him in the darkness, more convinced than ever that he hadn't forgotten a damn thing. Except, maybe, to make a move. "What'd you forget?"

He stepped closer. Close enough so his jeans brushed against hers. Their arms met, too, the contact unexpected because she hadn't seen it coming in the dim light. Cat flinched, caught off guard by the heart-stopping sensuality of such a simple touch. She'd been touched much more intimately by men before. But even the most evocative ones hadn't been able to inspire the heat she was feeling now.

"You think I intentionally left my keys so I'd have to come back and get them?"

"Keys, huh?"

"Why else would I have come back?" His tone dared her to tell the truth—to admit the heated images filling her mind.

Cat shifted, brushing her bare arm against his again. This time he was the one who hissed—softly, almost inaudibly—but she heard it. So, he, too, was feeling the energy snapping between them, so potent and heady.

The tension built. She was barely touching his forearm, the hard angle of his wrist, but she reacted as if she were caressing the most sensitive parts of his body. The hairs on her arm stood on end and the nerve endings there tingled. She couldn't even imagine what it would be like to touch him all over.

"Maybe you came back for a good-night kiss," she said, dying for it to be true.

A kiss. Surely one little kiss wasn't going to stop the world and ruin all her good intentions.

And you really think a kiss is going to be enough?

No. Probably not. But she wanted it, anyway. Right at this moment, she wanted it more than she wanted to save the bar.

He laughed softly. "What makes you think I'm the kind of guy who kisses on the first day?"

Because I want you to be? Instead, she replied, "There's something between us."

"Yes."

"You're attracted to me."

"Yes."

Cat licked her lips. "So what are you gonna do about it?"

He said nothing for a long, heady moment. Then he leaned even closer, close enough so she felt his warm breaths against her cheek. Smelled the aroma of warm cologne and warmer man.

"Kissing's very personal," he whispered.

She wobbled. Because his whisper had been right by her temple, so close she felt the brush of his lips. She tingled there. Everywhere.

"Very intimate."

This time, his words were accompanied by the soft, slight brush of his hand sliding up her arm. His palm just barely connected with her skin as he slid it from wrist to elbow, then higher, until his fingertips rested as light as a butterfly on her bare shoulder.

And suddenly she realized that he was seducing her. Not with anything as blatant as a kiss, but with these incredibly sensuous whispers, the almost-there touches that had her silently screaming for more. "Spence..."

"Shh," he said, coming closer, so his leg was almost between hers. Their thighs converged, sending a spiral of warm longing straight between hers. His long, smooth hair brushed against her cheek, his fingers still rested on her shoulders. His dark eyes glittered in the half light and she sensed the beating of his heart across the scant inch that separated her chest from his.

Every one of her senses roared to life, clamoring for more. Much more. She'd never been so aroused in her life. Never.

She was too weak to lift her arms around his neck. Too besotted to tilt her head back for his kiss. Too overwhelmed by the sensations battering her from every side to do much more than stand there and experience the intense awareness, the sound of his breath, the anticipation of his touch in the darkness.

"Please…"

Before she could say another word, he lowered his head and pressed one hot, erotic, open-mouthed kiss to the hollow of her throat. Cat's legs buckled. She grabbed for the nearest table, not sure she was going to be able to remain upright. "Oh, my God," she choked out.

Spence continued to delicately sample her skin as if tasting something delicious. "You know," he said softly, pulling only a breath away, "sometimes when you know something is going to be incredible, waiting for it makes it that much better."

He touched his lips to that hollow again, sliding them up the column of her throat in one smooth, delicate caress. And oh, Lord, he was right. Knowing how incredible— how explosive—their kiss would be when their mouths met, Cat practically groaned.

But just as he reached her chin—just as he built the anticipation of his lips on hers until she was as tense as a taut wire—he straightened and pulled away. And then he did the unthinkable. He stepped back, offered her one small, intimate smile, then turned around.

Cat could only watch, jaw hanging open, while he

jumped up onto the stage and grabbed for something sitting on one of the chairs there. A clink told her it was his keys. It was a miracle she could hear them, considering her breathing was louder than a freight train.

"Good night, Cat," he said as he stepped off the stage.

Watching in shock, she couldn't manage a single word. Not until after he walked by her, right out the door. He pulled it shut behind him and disappeared into the night.

For several long moments, she remained silent. When her vocal cords did start working again, the only word she could manage was one she was supposed to have stricken from her vocabulary. And it sure wasn't ladylike.

"I NEED THE SLUTTIEST PAIR of shoes you've got."

Cat's jaw dropped open and she gaped at Gracie, who stood at her door Saturday morning. Way too early Saturday morning.

"What time is it?"

"Ten."

Cat groaned and staggered back, clearing the way for her usually quiet friend to barrel in. Gracie owned Between The Covers, the book shop next door, and had apparently forgotten the cardinal rule: no banging on Cat's door at 10 a.m. on a Saturday when she'd been closing down the bar until three that morning.

It was a wonder she'd even heard Gracie's pounding, because she still felt half asleep. Not only because of the short duration of her night, but also because of the rather, uh, *interesting* dreams she'd had about a certain hot guitar player who'd aroused her nearly to the point of orgasm before walking out the night before.

He'd been naked in most of them. Naked and holding a jar of peanut butter.

"Cat, did you hear what I said? I need to borrow some shoes. The sluttiest ones in your closet."

Cat raised a hand to her chest. "Slut shoes? Moi?"

Gracie lifted one brow, just watching, until Cat grudgingly said, "Okay, slut shoes, *vous*?"

"Yes, me." Her tone said she wasn't kidding. Without another word, Gracie marched down the short hallway between Cat's living room and kitchen, heading toward the back of the small apartment. Once inside Cat's bedroom, she practically dove into the closet.

Cat followed. "You're serious?" she asked, leaning against the doorjamb, watching her friend dig frantically through her stockpile of footwear.

"Very. I want something high, strappy. Shoes that say I'm wicked and willing and sexy as can be."

Wow. This was so not Gracie. Not just the shoes, but the whole nervous, energetic frenzy. Gracie was the calm one of their foursome. The quiet, graceful one with her soft brown hair and lovely blue eyes. Not the one she'd expect to be on all fours in Cat's closet, flinging shoes over her shoulder one after another.

"Hate to remind you, but my feet are bigger than yours."

"Half a size. I'll stuff the toe."

With a chuckle, Cat knelt down to help look. There was a lot to look through. Cat had sort of a little thing for shoes. Actually, sort of a big thing for them. Imelda Marcos-size. Which anyone could tell with one look at the mountain of footwear in varying shades covering the entire floor of her closet.

"What color?" she asked, trying to narrow down the search.

"Black." Gracie brushed a strand of hair off her face, and

squared her shoulders, looking resolute. "I'm going to my ten-year reunion tonight and I want the kind of shoes that make men drool and women think catty, mean things about other women."

Gracie didn't have a catty, mean bone in her body, so Cat immediately took her request more seriously. "Okay, forget this stuff, we need to go up a level. And oh, sister, are you in luck, because I have got just what you need!"

Cat rose to her feet—staggered, really, since her bones hadn't yet achieved her brain's level of wakefulness. Standing on tiptoe, she reached up to the top shelf of her closet, where another dozen or so shoe boxes were stacked in neat rows. This was where she stashed the good stuff. The ones on the floor were the throwaways. Up here were the jewels in her collection.

She zoned in on the third stack, where the black shoes began, organized by heel height. It didn't take long to find the box she was looking for. "I fell in love with these on the Jimmy Choo Web site and ordered them last year."

Gracie's eyes widened. "Jimmy Choo?"

Cat nodded. "Yep. I think I owe someone a kidney, but it was so worth it because they're to die for. And they're a teensy bit small on me, so they might fit you just perfectly."

Of course, they could have been three sizes too small and Cat would have done a Cinderella's stepsister thing and worn them, anyway. If it came down to a choice between toes and Jimmy Choos, the shoes would win every time.

She wondered if Spence liked women in spiked heels.

And nothing else.

No. No more fantasies about the guy. After he'd walked out on her last night, she wasn't sure she'd ever let him back into her real life *or* her fantasy one.

Shrugging off the image, Cat watched Gracie nibble her lip in anticipation. Before taking off the lid, she cautioned, "You can't tell Laine about these, okay? She wouldn't understand that I considered it totally worthwhile to live on peanut butter sandwiches for a month so I could afford these."

Mmm. Peanut butter. That brought Spence right back to the forefront of her mind. Again. Dammit, he had no business being so desirable, not after the way he'd aroused her to insanity, then left her hanging there. She might never speak to him again, much less get personal with a jar of peanut butter.

Unless he kissed her throat again. Then she was a goner.

Gracie nodded. "Deal."

Cat removed the top and peeled back the paper, watching for Gracie's reaction.

Silent awe. They shared it for a few moments, gazing at the glory of the shoes, as would any other red-blooded American female. The other half of the population didn't get and never would get the shoe thing, but women of all ages, shapes and sizes would pause to pay homage to these things of beauty.

Then Gracie whispered, "Those are perfect!"

"Haute couture slut shoes," Cat said with pride.

"I owe you."

Cat shrugged. "Just don't knock on my door at 10 a.m. tomorrow to tell me how it went."

Gracie's pretty blue eyes suddenly shifted away, and Cat wondered exactly what the woman was up to. But she didn't pry. Everybody had secrets—including Cat. Besides, considering Gracie's bookstore was going to be every bit as out of business as Temptation, she figured the woman was entitled to her own private let-it-all-out party.

"I hear the place was packed last night," Gracie said. "Must have been some band you booked."

Cat looked away. "Uh huh. He was something else."

"He? A one-man band?"'

Cursing her dumb, sleepy, one-track brain, Cat said, "Oh, no, sorry, I meant they. They were something else."

Gracie wasn't buying it. "Who's the 'he'?"

Cat couldn't even try to come up with a cover story. "He's a drop-dead gorgeous bass player named Spence who is exactly the kind of guy Laine and my mother would have heart attacks over if I ever brought him around for dinner."

Nodding, Gracie put the lid back onto the shoe box, then gave Cat a tiny half smile.

"Then I'd say it's a good thing Laine and your mother are far, far away."

DYLAN DECIDED BEFORE leaving his house in Tremont Saturday afternoon that come hell or high water, before the night was out, he'd have kissed Cat Sheehan. *Really* kissed her.

One kiss. He'd deliver the kiss he'd all but promised both of them last night. The one worth waiting nine years for.

Then, and only then, would he be able to tell her the truth: who he was, how she knew him. He'd come clean about where he lived, what he really did. All of it.

Except, perhaps for the song. He wasn't quite ready to share that, or his memories of the bonfire. But everything else was getting laid out on the table.

Too bad *he* wasn't.

"Knock it off," he told himself, knowing he'd better not let his mind go down that road. Not if he wanted to be comfortable in his jeans for the rest of the night.

He forced himself to focus on his confession. Honesty

was the key. He'd tell her everything, right down to that moment in the cafeteria when her pretty white teeth had bitten into his apple and taken a chunk out of his heart.

Okay, strike that, too. He'd mention the apple part, but not necessarily his heart. Because he certainly wasn't the same nerdy fifteen-year-old kid he'd been then. He now knew his teenage infatuation with Cat had been merely that…infatuation. First love, when love had seemed to be the only explanation because of the goofy smile that always came to his lips whenever he saw her walk by. Or the way time had seemed to stand still whenever he'd heard her laugh. Not to mention the way he'd made himself believe he was the only person who saw the serious, lonely side of the most popular girl in school.

Then it had felt like love. *Now* he recognized it as a raging case of hormones. Those immature feelings had nothing to do with adult emotions, and it would be silly to bring them up. He'd embarrass them both, particularly when the keen interest and heat faded from Cat's eyes as she realized he *wasn't* the dangerous, reckless guy she'd always seemed to date back in high school.

Not even close.

He was still a brain, still quiet, and still kept to himself when he wasn't on stage. As for dangerous? Well, he was about as ruthless and tough as a guppy. The only part of the wild side he walked on with regularity these days was when he appeared with the Four G's.

And considering what the name of their band stood for, that *wasn't* very wild at all.

Dylan arrived in downtown Kendall a little early Saturday, hoping for some alone time with Cat before the bar crowd drifted in. Actually, he arrived a *lot* early. It was only five and they weren't due to play until eight. "Too early," he told himself. "She'll think you're a stalker."

He sat in his car in the parking garage a block away from the bar. He'd parked here instead of in the small lot behind her building for one reason: because he didn't want Cat to know he drove an expensive, boring, imported sedan. Just like he didn't want her to know he lived in a moderately pricey neighborhood in Tremont, in a large, modern three-bedroom house, whose only claim to being hip was the incredible sound system he'd had built into it during construction.

She wouldn't understand any of it. Cat wouldn't be able to associate the car, the house—and certainly not his job as a software designer and consultant—with the laid-back band member she'd been coming on to last night.

Coming on to. Yeah. She had been. They both knew it. Like they both knew he could have taken things a hell of a lot further last night if his conscience hadn't kicked in and demanded he leave.

Which was why he knew he had to take his shot and kiss her, just once, before telling her the truth. Because if he knew Cat—and he did—she would *not* be coming on to a guy she thought was a boring software geek who had his oil changed every three thousand miles and invested in tech stocks.

Besides, it wasn't as if he'd be taking anything she didn't want to give, judging by the way they'd danced around the sizzling awareness last night. Only a fool wouldn't act on that awareness at least once before it disappeared forever.

Hoisting his guitar case over his shoulder, he hoofed it to Temptation, walking through the front door to find the place pretty much deserted. Though it was just after five on a Saturday, not one pub diner sat at any of the tables munching on a greasy burger. No hard-core, all-day weekend drinkers were staring up at the television, where a ball game was going on.

The only person around was Cat.

Who was lying flat on her back on top of the bar.

He grinned, unable to help it, and quietly approached her. Wondering what she was doing, he stood in the shadows several feet away, just watching. With a sigh he could hear from here, Cat lifted a pencil, took aim and threw it straight up. Following the pencil's ascent with his gaze, he saw it join several others sticking into the ceiling over the bar.

Somebody had obviously been bored today.

"I think it took Mulder about three seasons of *The X-Files* to get that many pencils on the ceiling of his office."

She didn't even look over. "Took me about three hours."

"You know, a fly swatter would probably be more effective."

She chuckled. "If I were going after Texas houseflies, I'd be using a shotgun, not pencils."

He walked to the bar, putting his guitar case on the floor beside it. Sliding onto a stool, he smiled down at her. "Bad day?"

She rolled her eyes. "You're the second person who's walked in since we opened at one. And the first one was a construction guy asking to use the bathroom."

He frowned. "You didn't shoot him, did you?"

Cat finally looked over, her eyes twinkling in sudden merriment. "Not even with a pencil." Then she looked up at the ceiling again. "It's not his fault. He just works for the bureaucrats—he doesn't make the lousy decisions."

He gave an exaggerated sigh. "Whew. Because I still don't have a shovel handy."

A tiny grin tugged at her lips. "You'd help me bury the body?"

He leaned closer over the bar, looking down at her beautiful face. "Oh, absolutely."

Their eyes met, their stares holding for a long, thick moment. Cat's grin faded and so did Dylan's.

That awareness was back. Made more intense by her provocative position—flat on her back. And his position—above her. They were both remembering the last time they'd seen each other, right here, during their relatively innocent exchange that had been so incredibly intimate.

Cat was the one who looked away first, though the color in her cheeks made a lie of her casual tone. "Well, thanks anyway, but I haven't murdered anyone yet."

Dylan followed her lead, ignoring the sexual attraction dancing so strongly between them. She obviously wanted to pretend last night hadn't happened. That was fine with him.

For now.

Straightening a bit on his stool, he asked, "You have fought this road issue as far as you can, I assume?"

She nodded. "Yeah. There's nothing more to do. The city has named the date and time of demolition. We have to be out of here by June 30 at the very latest."

He shook his head. "I'm really sorry, Cat."

She picked up another pencil from a pile next to her jean-clad hip. "I'm handling it." This time when she threw it, Dylan was much closer. Close enough to see the way her tight, sleeveless red shirt pulled even tighter across her body as she flexed her arm. And a tempting, creamy strip of skin across her belly where her shirt pulled free of the waistband of her white jeans.

She didn't even seem aware of how each graceful movement accentuated the soft curve of her shoulder, the vulnerable, pale skin of her neck. Nor how she was affecting him. Which, for a woman as sensually aware as Cat, indicated the depth of her bad mood.

He glanced away, trying to keep his breathing slow and steady. Swallowing hard, he forced his attention back to their conversation. "So what are you going to do after you close?"

She shrugged. "Not sure yet."

"I assume the city's giving you a fair price for the building? The law requires them to give you market value and downtown properties sell for a good amount."

Cat looked over again, raising a curious brow. Dylan realized he'd sounded a little more like a lawyer than a laid-back musician. He gave her a self-deprecating look. "I watch *Law & Order*."

"Well, that's good to know, in case I do murder the next construction worker who comes in looking for a bathroom." Grinning, she abruptly sat up on the bar and swiveled around so her legs dangled off the front of it. She was close. So close her hip almost touched his arm. And the awareness factor shot up a notch.

He tightened his fingers into a fist on his lap and forced a casual tone. "You never answered my question about the sale."

"The city is paying a good amount for the land, but since my mother and uncle still own the building, the bulk of it will go to them."

Ouch. He hadn't figured on that. He'd assumed Cat owned the place and would be financially stable after the shutdown. Stable enough to stick around town for a while.

"I'm hopeful, though," she admitted softly, "that I'll have enough to help me go to school part-time." She looked as if she regretted it the minute the words left her mouth.

"School? You want to go back to college?"

"Basically *start* college. I think I lasted one-and-a-half semesters at the community college before I dropped out. But I'm ready for it now."

"What do you want to do?"

She looked away. "You'll laugh."

"No," he replied, meaning it, "I won't."

Lifting her hand to her mouth and almost covering her lips, she mumbled, "I'd like to teach high school."

Dylan coughed a bit as the air in his throat turned a little grainy. Talk of high school cut way too close for comfort.

"You're laughing," she snapped.

"No, I'm absolutely *not* laughing. I think that's fantastic and you'd be a great teacher. Being able to deal with people from all walks of life, to listen and advise and befriend anybody who pulls up a stool at your bar is a remarkable bonus for someone who wants to teach teenagers."

She didn't look entirely convinced, but finally, she shrugged. "Well, who knows. Right now all I've done is call for an application. I haven't even visited the university campus."

"You should. You definitely should."

She again lowered her head, shielding her expressive face with her long hair, appearing uncomfortable at having started the conversation. "We'll see. There's so much to do in the meantime, and without anybody else around, it's not going to be easy."

"So why *aren't* they here helping with all this going-out-of-business stuff?"

"There's a good question. God, all my life I've been waiting for my family to treat me like a responsible adult who can do more than pour beer. Be careful what you wish for, right? Because now they're all gone and I'm handling everything by myself."

She let out a tiny laugh—definitely forced—which made Dylan reassess her mood. Cat being alone in the bar when he'd arrived hadn't merely been about a lack of customers. It had somehow symbolized much more. As if she were totally alone in her life. And more than a little unhappy about it.

Which got him thinking about those occasional lonely moments he'd witnessed in high school. The other Cat only he had seen.

Judging by the way she crossed her arms and looked away, she didn't want to continue that conversation, so Dylan looked up at the ceiling. "You gonna leave them hanging there?"

She shrugged. "The wrecking ball can handle a few pencils, I think." Then she added, "This looks pathetic, I know, but I've always wanted to do it. I used to imagine lying on top of the bar when I was a kid. I figured I might as well do it while I have the chance. Nobody was around to see."

Since she was now sitting above him, instead of lying below him, Dylan had to look up again to answer. He tried to focus only on her face, but it was tough with her curvy body so close to his. Her breasts were at eye level and it was all he could do to keep his stare firmly above them. "Anything else you've always wanted to do in here?"

She looked around the room, studying the groupings of tables, the small stage, the jukebox. Then, with a small nod, she admitted, "Yeah. A few things."

The secretive smile playing about her lips made him very curious about what kinds of things. When she didn't elaborate, he prodded, "One of them have anything to do with that stage?"

She nibbled her lip and nodded. "Uh huh. And different colored spotlights."

The wicked glint in her eye told him she wasn't necessarily thinking of performing on that stage, but he still had to ask, "Are you a closet singer?"

"A shower singer," she admitted. "A tone-deaf shower singer. Even worse than Tess."

"Tess?"

A tiny frown appeared on Cat's brow. "She's one of our waitresses. She had to leave town unexpectedly."

Sensing the subject was a sore one, he didn't ask for details. "So what do you see yourself doing on the stage?"

Her eyes flared and her lips parted as she drew in a slow, deep breath. The intensity shot up, as he imagined Cat, naked, highlighted in the colored spotlights she'd mentioned. Having hot, erotic sex on the stage, bathed in all that light.

"I'm not sure I'm ready to share that particular fantasy."

Dylan shook his head and managed a rueful grin. "To be honest with you, I'm not sure I'm ready to hear it."

"Chicken?"

"Self-preservationist. I have to go up there and perform in a couple of hours. And it won't be easy if I'm imagining you the way I'm picturing you right now."

His husky words dared her to go further in this sexy game of supposition—to ask him what he was picturing. But Cat didn't take the bait this time. Just as well. If she confirmed his most heated imaginings, Dylan didn't think he'd be able to stop at the one simple kiss he planned to have from her in a very short while.

Reaching into a bowl on the bar, he grabbed a fistful of peanuts and tossed a few into his mouth. A stall for time, but it worked. Because eventually his pulse stopped racing and his groin obeyed his brain's command to go back into standby mode instead of running things, as it wanted to.

"So," he asked, "What else do you plan to do before you shut the doors for the last time? Tap dancing on the tables?"

She snickered. "Tap dancing? If my mother had tried to put me in a pair of tap shoes as a kid, I would have used them to kick down the nearest door and escape."

Sounded like something the wild young Cat would have done. Sounded like something the *adult* Cat would do now.

"But I might just have to dance on top of this bar one of these nights," she added, stroking the smooth wood surface with the palm of one hand. "To something slow and smoky."

Smoky. A word most people wouldn't think of in connection with music, but one which made perfect sense to Dylan. It was sensual, perfectly apt for this woman who continued to caress the wood with lingering strokes of her long, delicate fingers.

Unable to resist, he smoothed his own hand over the mahogany, feeling what she was feeling. Experiencing the same touch Cat so obviously savored.

It was smooth. Warm. Slick. Strong and solid. And probably held a great many memories for the young woman sitting there, touching the surface of something that meant so much to her. Something she was being forced to give away.

His gut twisted. Cat revealed so much, without even saying a word. The way she tenderly rubbed the tips of her fingers over a scratch here, a gouge there, revealed the depth of her emotions.

It had to be like losing a part of herself.

God, he wished there were something he could do to help her through it. Then he realized there was. Because until he'd walked through the door, she'd been completely and utterly alone.

And now she wasn't.

"So," he finally said, "is there anything else you have to get out of your system before you move?"

She cocked her head, thinking about it. "Well, I fully intend to sunbathe naked in the garden out back at least once before they kick me out."

The air in his mouth suddenly tasted thick and dusty. Dylan couldn't help coughing a bit at the mental image of Cat lying naked in the sunlight, glorious, pagan and seductive.

"Sorry, did I shock you?" she asked, not sounding a bit sorry. "You don't look like the type to be easily shocked."

No, the wild, up-for-anything rock and roller she saw when she looked at him wouldn't be easily shocked.

And he wasn't. The images cascading in his brain weren't shocking. They were…intoxicating.

"I'm not shocked," he said softly, letting her see the heat in his eyes. "Just picturing…the possibilities."

This time, Cat was the one who appeared a little breathless. Her lips parted and she nervously licked at them, eliciting another nearly silent groan of reaction from him. Dylan covered the sound by clearing his throat.

"Oh," she said.

"Feel free to let me know when you're going to be checking off all the items on your to-do list," he said, not quite achieving the light tone he'd been going for. "I'd be happy to keep watch."

"You mean you'd be happy to watch."

"What if I gave my Scout's honor not to even sneak a peek?"

A grin tugged at her mouth. "Then I think I'd be terribly disappointed."

"You flirting with me again?"

Raising a hand to her chest, she said, in feigned innocence, "Flirting? Me? When have I ever flirted with you?"

"Uh, I think last night when you were working the bar there was some definite flirting."

"No, last night when I was working the bar there was some definite foot-in-mouth disease going around."

"I liked that about you."

"That I came across as a stammering idiot?"

No. That *he'd* made her react like a stammering idiot. But he wasn't about to admit that. "It was cute."

"Puppies are cute." She sounded disgruntled. "I prefer to be a sleek, mysterious feline."

"Hence the name."

"Speaking of names, you going to tell me the rest of yours?" she asked.

He could. Here was the golden opportunity to jog Cat's memory and see what happened. He almost did it, wanting to see something—a spark of recognition, anything—on Cat's face. Only one thing stopped him.

He still hadn't gotten his kiss.

"Spence is enough."

She shrugged. "Suit yourself." Then, swinging her legs back and forth over the edge of the bar, she asked, "So why'd you show up here so early tonight, Spence?"

She sounded friendly, almost glad that he had. Not suspicious at all. Which made him suddenly feel uncomfortable for not being honest with her. He really needed to come clean. But the only words he could manage were, "No particular reason. I can leave if I'm keeping you away from any pressing…pencil-tossing."

She shook her head, sending that long cascade of golden hair bouncing over her shoulders. A sudden rush of longing flashed through him, making his hands tingle at the thought of burying them in all her glorious hair. And he refocused on his goal: one kiss. One kiss before he lost his chance with her forever.

"So, do you want me to go?" he asked, his voice low but intense.

"No," she replied, suddenly sounding much less jaunty and much more serious. "I think I want you to stay."

4

CAT HAD BEEN TRYING since the previous night to convince herself that a long-haired, dark-eyed musician was not someone she could allow on her radar, much less into her life. She'd been hammering the point home in her brain with every toss of a pencil into the ceiling, building up strength to be cool, aloof and reserved when he showed up that night.

Not bloody likely.

Because he'd gone and shown up early, looking all sexy, scruffy, dangerous and hot, and her good intentions had gone right out the window, along with her common sense.

Now things had gotten worse. Because now, when she was truly alone with him, she had to concede it wasn't mere sexual attraction she felt for the man. She liked him. Liked spending time with him. Liked the husky timbre of his voice and the way his eyes crinkled when he smiled.

Mostly, she liked the way he looked at her: as if he could see past every facade she'd erected, into the deep, innermost woman known to no one else in the world.

His intensity charged her up like nothing else. More than his sex appeal, more than his incredible looks, or his great sense of humor, it was the certainty that he knew exactly what made Cat Sheehan tick that she found nearly irresistible.

So, for the next hour or so, she didn't even try to resist. It wasn't *too* dangerous—after all, though they were alone, somebody could walk into Temptation at any moment. She couldn't get into too much trouble.

Yeah, right. She was the one walking into Temptation. Because if he so much as lifted a finger to touch her cheek, she'd almost surely be diving into his lap.

The realization should have been enough to make her get off the bar, walk behind it and busy herself doing nonsense work. Anything to give him the message that she was not interested.

It didn't. Instead, she set aside thoughts of where she'd be living next month, of the changes she was supposed to make, the swearing off of guys with no future and danger in their every movement. And she allowed herself to enjoy his company.

Probably would have been safer to just leap on him, kiss the taste out of his mouth and give in to the attraction. Because the whole liking thing seemed infinitely more dangerous.

Still, how could she *not* like him? He had a wicked sense of humor, kept up with her in the one-liners and had been incredibly understanding when she'd gone on a long ramble about the loss of her family legacy.

He wasn't too chatty, but his carefully chosen words both amused and intrigued her. Especially because every time she tried to learn more about the man, he managed to change the subject.

Curiosity. It was Cat's downfall. Hers was now killing her.

She wanted to know him better. Who he really was. Where he was from. What made him tick. What his amazing mouth tasted like.

"So," he said, interrupting her heated musings, "since

you're not exactly packing them in, why don't you take a break. Let me wait on you for a change? I make a damn good margarita."

Cat's jaw dropped. "You want to wait on *me*?"

Nodding, Spence rose from his stool and walked around behind the bar. "When's the last time you sat out there and let someone make you a drink?"

Uh, never, that she could recall. By the time she was old enough to drink, she was already working at the pub, and was running it—with Laine's help—a year later. "I'm not sure I've ever sat on the receiving side of the bar," she admitted, looking down from her perch. Realizing it was one more thing she could do that she'd never done before, she hopped down and slid onto the stool Spence had just vacated.

Tapping her finger with mock impatience, she said, "What's a person gotta do to get some service around here?"

"What'll it be?"

With a saucy tilt of her head, Cat said, "Maybe I want a Slippery Nipple."

His eyes flashed, but his jaw didn't drop in shock. Instead, he leaned an elbow on the bar, and leaned over it. "Well then, maybe you should take off your shirt and I'll see what I can do."

Hers was the jaw that dropped. "It's a *drink*. Irish cream and butterscotch schnapps."

Raising a brow in complete innocence, he said, "Well, how could I *possibly* have known that?"

The tiny grin he couldn't hide made Cat shake her head in rueful amusement. He'd turned the tables on her. "You got me."

"You started it."

Yeah, she had, to her dismay. Because, wow, the echo of

this man's voice telling her to take off her shirt was going to be ringing in her head all night.

"Most people don't know what it is," she said, hoping he wouldn't notice the weakness of her voice. "Women are usually too embarrassed to order it from male bartenders. And guys don't drink it."

"I dunno," he said. "Sounded kind of interesting to me. Warm. Sweet. Creamy." His voice was a little thick as he continued. "Might be something I'd like to try late some night."

Cat's body immediately reacted to the suggestive words and tone. Not to mention the way his gaze shifted so he could cast a lazy, appreciative look down the front of her body.

Drawing in a slow, steady breath, she shifted in her seat again, the stool hard and uncomfortable against her suddenly very tender bottom half. Her nipples grew taut and tight, achy, as she pictured Spence having his drink…sucking and licking it right off her breasts. Just as he'd intended her to.

"Now, do you really want a Slippery Nipple?" His tone was pure velvet. Pure seduction. "Because I'd be happy to take care of that for you."

Oh, God, yes!

If her breasts could speak, that's exactly what they'd have screamed. Because she was dying for him to kiss her, stroke her, run his tongue in lazy circles around her nipple before taking it into his mouth and sucking. Hard, fast. Deep.

A tiny sigh escaped her lips and she closed her eyes briefly. When she opened them again, she realized Spence had straightened up, giving her some space.

The sensible Cat—the one who knew somebody could walk through the door at any moment, and that if she continued with this sensual game, she might do something really dangerous—answered. "Margarita will be fine."

He nodded. "Frozen or on the rocks?"

"Rocks," she ordered, unable to do much more than stare as Spence got to work squeezing limes and grabbing for their best tequila. Triple Sec. Then he proved he really knew what he was doing and reached for the Cointreau.

"Salt?"

A margarita without salt? Horrors. "Of course."

Finishing her drink, he slid it across the broad surface of the bar, looking pleased with himself. When she brought the drink to her lips and sipped it, she knew why. "This is good."

"Damn good," he said.

No false modesty here. She liked that about him, too. And she wondered what else he might be damn good at.

She sipped again, using the tart iciness of her drink to cool off the heat of her thoughts. Because other than his bartending and musical skills, she had no business wondering what else Spence was good at. No business at all.

"So no guy has ever made you a drink?"

"Most people are scared to serve a bartender," she admitted. "I guess it would kinda be like somebody cooking for a chef."

"You're *that* good?"

Cat wasn't falsely modest, either. "Yeah." Then, with a wry laugh, she admitted, "And, of course, most of the guys I've dated wouldn't know how to *spell* margarita, much less make one."

"No Einsteins in your little black book, hmm?"

"Uh, no."

"Why not?"

Why not indeed? She almost told him the truth. She was the one who usually threw up barriers with smarter, everyday nice guys who occasionally came into her world. Laine had once said it was because Cat had self-esteem issues—not about her looks, but about her personality and brains. As if thinking of herself as the black sheep of the Sheehan family had made her think she wasn't qualified to seek out a nice, respectable guy.

Cat didn't know much about psychology, but she sometimes wondered if Laine was on to something. Because Cat did have a history of sabotaging any relationship with a decent man that looked as if it could actually go anywhere. It seemed safer to stick with the bad boys because there was no danger of getting her heart trampled on when they walked out the door. If she started out expecting them to go, she couldn't be devastated when they did.

Wrong. Don't think like that.

Just because practically everybody had left in the past—through death, retirement, remarriage or wildfire adventures—didn't mean everyone would in her future. One way or another, she was going to convince herself it was possible to find someone to share her life. Someone normal and safe who'd actually want to stick around.

Someone totally unlike the incredible guy she'd been flirting with since last night.

She sighed heavily, then stiffened her shoulders in resolve. Dammit, she was going to change if it killed her. And she had to admit it, watching the way Spence moved with such casual, male grace—knowing she would never *really* see what he could do—it just might.

"No time for any little black book these days," she finally said. "I've been focused totally on the business for the past few years."

"And now?" he asked.

Now? What now? Well, wasn't that the question of the hour? Of the year, really. What was she going to do now?

"Let's talk about you for a while. Why don't you tell me about her?" Cat asked, surprising even herself when she voiced the question.

"Who?"

The woman you loved. The one you still think about, judging by the way you sing her song.

Instead, she explained, "The woman who inspired the song you wrote. The one with the fire in her eyes."

Spence said nothing for a moment, simply looking at her intently. Cat forced her stare to remain steady, as if she was merely curious, making idle conversation. Instead of prying deeply into this man's heart—his romantic past.

She had no business asking, she had less business knowing.

But she couldn't help it.

"She was someone I knew a long time ago," he admitted.

"She broke your heart?"

He laughed softly. "She never knew it was hers to break." With a shrug, he added, "She hardly even noticed me."

Unrequited love? Didn't seem possible—not with this man. What woman could have him in her life and not notice him? Not be overwhelmed by all that confidence, that sexy, seething attractiveness? "She must have been an idiot."

His eyes twinkled. "No. She was just...out of my league."

Oh, now she got it. He'd fallen for some snotty rich bitch who'd thought a down-and-out musician was beneath her.

Isn't that what you've been trying to tell yourself?

No. No, it wasn't. Spence wasn't beneath her. Ha. If

anything, she *wanted* him beneath her. On top of her. Anywhere she could have him.

Don't go there, Cat.

No, her need to keep some kind of barriers between her and the hunky musician had nothing to do with class or status, and everything to do with her need to change direction in her life.

He was just the wrong guy at the wrong time.

Lifting her glass, she finished her drink in two deep sips, smacking her lips together when she was done. Spence watched her intently.

"What?"

"You liked it."

"I liked it."

He leaned across the bar, resting on his elbow. "So I guess I'm gonna get a pretty big...tip."

The way he said the word *tip* made her think he had something other than money in mind. When he caught the base of her margarita glass between two fingers and pulled it out of the way so he could lean closer, she began to figure out what it was.

"If you wanted a taste, you could have made your own," she said breathily.

"I don't want my own drink, Cat," he murmured. "But I definitely want a taste."

"A kiss for a tip?"

"Uh-huh. One kiss."

Oh, God, one kiss. That was like saying one potato chip or one M&M. Some things were just meant to be done in multiples.

She should tell him to shove off. Should send him out the door and order him not to come back until showtime.

Instead, she scowled and answered with the first words

that came to her lips. "If you kiss my throat and then walk away from me again, you're going to be wearing what's left of this drink."

He laughed softly. "I have no intention of wearing your drink. And no intention of walking away until I get my kiss."

Her heart raced as Spence touched her cheek with the tip of his index finger and tilted her head up. He didn't try to grab her, didn't force her toward him, but the touch of his finger on her face was magnetic. She leaned closer. Closer. Until their lips were a whisper apart.

Then, suddenly, there was nothing between them at all. *A kiss, it's just a kiss*, she tried to remind herself.

But it was no use. Because the moment Spence's warm, tender mouth met hers, she was lost. Lost in his taste, in the warmth of the breaths they shared. In the slip of his tongue against her bottom lip, which made her whimper with the need for more. He complied, lazily licking at the crease between her lips until she parted them for him and met his tongue with her own.

Soon all thought ceased and sensation took over. Sweet and hot and silky smooth, the kiss went on and on, a mating of lips and tongue as intimate as any embrace Cat had ever experienced, though they touched in no other place.

Whoever said a kiss was just a kiss had never been kissed by this man. Because with Spence, a kiss was flat-out lovemaking. He made hot, tender love to her mouth until she began to quiver, to shake almost with the need for this to go on and on and on.

But it didn't. It couldn't. Nothing perfect could go on forever, and he finally—regretfully—lifted his mouth away from hers. The heat emanating from his eyes warmed her all over again, promising her more. So much more. Later.

Cat couldn't stand it. She wanted more *now*. She leaned forward again, silently begging him to kiss her.

And promptly fell off the damn stool.

DYLAN WATCHED Cat gently touch a fresh bag of ice to her forehead, feeling incredibly guilty for causing her pain. "Any better?" he asked.

"My head or my ego?"

He chuckled, not answering that one.

The two of them were in the tiny kitchen of Cat's apartment, upstairs from the bar. They'd retreated there immediately after her accident. Fortunately, Cat's part-time waitress—Dinah—had arrived for work and was on duty downstairs. Dinah had walked in just in time to see Cat fall off her stool and whack her head on the edge of the bar. So, at least she didn't think Dylan was some kind of abuser.

Good thing, because Cat was sporting both a lump on her forehead and a fat lip. She looked downright disreputable…as if she'd been in a bar fight.

And she still looked every bit as beautiful as she did the day she'd stolen his apple.

"Feeling better?" he asked, watching with concern while she rubbed the pack of ice back and forth over the small lump, already lightly bruised.

She shook her head.

"Do you need some aspirin or something?"

"I'm not in pain," she admitted grudgingly. "But my humiliation quota has been just about used up."

"It could have happened to anyone."

Sighing, she leaned back and rested her head against one of the upper cabinets. A bit of condensation from the bagged ice slipped down her temple, disappearing into the fine, golden hair just above her ear. Dylan drew in a deep breath, then slowly released it, reminding himself that she was hurting. Picturing slow, seductive droplets of water slowly riding across every curve and indentation of her body was not very gentlemanly.

Neither was watching the way her small pink tongue kept sliding out of her mouth, delicately testing the tenderness of the small lump on her bottom lip.

Clenching his fists and tightening his jaw, Dylan tore his attention away from her face. He did not need to think about Cat's lips—her soft lips, which had kissed him back with such erotic tenderness. Nor about her sweet tongue and delicious mouth, which he'd explored so thoroughly a little while ago.

He didn't know what might have happened if she hadn't fallen. If he'd have dived back in for another kiss—coming right over the top of the bar if need be. Because one thing was for damn sure—one kiss had *not* been enough. Now, having kissed her, he knew the only thing that would satisfy him would be making love to this woman.

"How do you manage to bring out my formerly well-disguised klutz tendencies?" she asked, sounding more amused than annoyed.

Crossing his arms, he leaned one hip against the counter on which Cat was sitting. "The stool was old and wobbly."

"My *legs* were wobbly."

Dylan couldn't help his first reaction—pleasure that his kiss had made her weak in the legs. Or his second—to cast an instant glance toward those long, slim legs. That was when he noticed the flecks of red there, stark and blatant against the white fabric of her jeans. "Uh, hate to tell you this, but it looks like your bloody lip did a little more damage."

Cat followed his stare and groaned. "Dammit, these are brand-new," she muttered.

"You should put something on the stains before they set," he said, figuring she would dab some stain remover on it while she still wore the jeans.

Not that she'd...she wouldn't...

But she did. Before he could say another word, Cat had dropped her bag of ice and hopped off the counter. Kicking her sneakers off her feet, she unsnapped, unzipped, and wriggled out of her jeans while he stood there, watching, wide-eyed and speculative.

As if she'd forgotten he was even in the room, she turned to the sink and put her jeans under some running water. That left him staring at a quite delectable view from behind. Her thick blond hair flowed halfway down her back, bright against her red top. His breathing grew shallow as he focused on her long, bare legs—graceful and slim and soft-looking. Then he allowed himself to glance at the barely covered curves of her bottom, clad only in a teeny pair of white nylon panties that barely qualified as underwear.

Could have been worse, he supposed as he tried to control a shudder of pure, undiluted want. She could have been a thong woman. Though, only in his immediate circumstances would that have been a bad thing.

· Then he noticed a swirl of color peeking up from the hem of her panties. Cat had a tattoo. A sexy-as-hell, breath-stealing tattoo. Blues and greens created delicate patterns on the small, vulnerable part of her back, right above her delectable cheeks, and he realized he was looking at a butterfly's wings unfurled in a delicate spiral. The cacophony of delicate color and vulnerable skin begged to be explored. With his mouth.

"Is it cold water for blood, or hot?" Cat asked, looking over her shoulder just in time to catch him staring at her ass. Her face pinkened and she slowly turned around.

That's when things went from bad to worse.

A saint would have looked, and Dylan was no saint. He allowed himself about three seconds of wicked visual indulgence, during which he noticed every detail. The jut of her hip. The wide swath of pale, perfect skin between the bottom hem of her shirt and the top of her nearly-there panties. The thinness of the nylon. The tiny bit of elastic scraping just above a shadow of curls visible through the fabric.

Dylan's pulse skipped a few beats. Then, using every bit of strength he had, he forced his eyes to shut, his imagination to shut *down*, and his libido to shut *off*.

When he opened his eyes again, he expected to see an empty room—expected Cat to have darted out for clothes.

She hadn't moved an inch. She simply watched him, silently, a hint of challenge evident by the slight quirk of her lips.

He groaned, low in his throat, and gave her a warning look. "Cat…"

"I don't usually whip off my clothes in front of strangers," she said, taking a step away from the sink toward the middle of the room. Toward him.

"We're not strangers," he pointed out, taking a step of his own. One step toward insanity.

"But really, I've got bikinis that are smaller." She sounded a little defensive. Not to mention breathless.

He risked another step. "Uh-huh." Raking one hot glance from her face down to her toes, he bit out, "Probably not quite as sheer, though."

Cat's eyes widened. Even from here, a few feet away, he could hear the rasp of her choppy breaths, could see the color rise in her cheeks and a sparkle of excitement glitter in her eyes. "So," she whispered, "I suppose I should go get some other clothes."

They each took one more step. Now he was less than a foot away from her. Less than twelve inches. Easily within arm's reach of all the delightful places on her body that he longed to touch. He kept his hands at his sides through sheer force of will. "You don't have to on my account."

One of her fine blond eyebrows lifted. "A gentleman might have turned his back."

Tilting his head to the side, he responded, "Whatever made you think I was a gentleman?"

His hand reached out before his brain sent the message not to, and within an instant he was touching her hip, then tugging her forward. Trailing his fingertips along the edge of the elastic, he caressed that soft, intimate skin between her stomach and heaven, until Cat literally gasped and quivered beneath his hand.

"Spence...

"Obviously you don't have bikini bottoms smaller than these. Because I can definitely see below your tan line."

She glanced down and made a funny little hissing sound. Probably because of the intensely seductive way his dark hand looked against the smooth flesh well below her belly.

Closing her eyes, Cat dropped her head back and arched toward him, just the tiniest bit, inviting more. More heat. More intensity. More danger.

More of his hand.

He slipped one fingertip below the panties and slid it into her curls, closing his own eyes and echoing her moan of pleasure. She was incredibly soft, incredibly welcoming, and he tangled another finger in that warm thatch. Unable to resist, he leaned down to taste the vulnerable skin on her jaw, then her chin and her throat, touching her ever so lightly all the while. Dipping close, but not going too far to turn back.

As much as he wanted to, he didn't kiss her. He couldn't... not with her tender-looking lip. And not without torturing himself even more.

"Please touch me," she said on a shaky moan.

"I am touching you," he whispered against the corner of her mouth. The uninjured corner.

"Touch me *here*," she ordered. She took him by surprise then, arching into his hand, until his fingers connected with hot, wet womanly flesh.

"Oh, yes," she cried, blocking out the sound of his own hopeless grunt of pleasure.

God, she felt amazing. Slick and silky smooth. Warm and wet and welcoming.

"Yes, yes," she muttered. Reaching up, she tangled her hands in his hair and tugged his mouth to hers, taking the kiss he hadn't given her.

He was careful, licking delicately around her sore, then letting his tongue tangle with hers in a deep, hungry mating.

She continued to move, to arch, to quiver, inviting him even farther. Dylan couldn't resist. He slowly slid one finger into her hot, tight channel, savoring her cries of pleasure almost as much as he savored the tightness of her skin against his own.

He touched her deep inside, then withdrew, only to ease in again, setting a slow, steady rhythm of lovemaking with his hand. The flicks of his thumb on her clit and his tongue in her mouth soon matched the thrusts of his finger, until there was nothing but sensation. For both of them

The pleasure intensified...for him as well as her, until Dylan was as hungry for her release as Cat. His own would have to wait. Though he was hard enough to burst out of his jeans, there was no way things could get that far. Not yet. So for now, he focused on her, determined to make her come in a powerful explosion of ecstasy. And to watch her do it.

Cat's moans grew louder, finally turning into orgasmic cries of release. Dylan couldn't contain a masculine smile of accomplishment, because seeing Cat go all the way was almost as good as climaxing himself.

Almost.

She shook and shuddered, sagging against him while he sampled the soft skin of her jaw and her neck. He continued to make lazy circles with his fingers, enjoying the drenching feel of her, knowing she was still aroused, in spite of her orgasm.

"I wanna taste your tattoo," he whispered against her earlobe, forcing the words out of his tight throat. "I want to turn you around and strip off these silly things you call underwear and get down on my knees to kiss and lick every inch of it."

She gasped and jerked against him. "Oh, God."

And then she came again. Just like that.

He'd barely had time to wrap his mind around it— around her incredibly passionate responses, when he heard someone yelling from outside her apartment.

"Cat," a voice called, "you okay? It's getting kinda crazy down there." The words were accompanied by a sharp rap on the front door.

Cat's eyes flew open, and Dylan immediately looked across her tiny living room to the door. "Is it locked?" he asked, regretfully pulling away from her and rearranging her panties.

Nodding her head, she cleared her throat. "I'm fine, Dinah. Give me five more minutes, okay? Then I'll be back down."

He watched her hold her breath as they both listened for—and finally heard—the waitress's footsteps walking away toward the stairs.

"Close one," he said with a tiny smile.

"Close? It was a little more than close for me," she replied, sounding a bit stunned.

"You complaining?"

"Do I look crazy?" she asked, cocking her head to one side.

He grinned. "Good. Because I have to admit, I got a hell of a charge out of it, too."

Cat straightened, smoothing her shirt, then running a hand through her hair. Drawing in a few deep breaths, as if trying to clear her head or calm herself down, she finally said, "It was incredible. But…unexpected."

"Definitely. So when can we expect to do it again?"

His words surprised a laugh out of her, but it quickly faded. "Spence…I…wow, what do I say to someone who just did *that* to me, but hasn't even seen me naked?"

"We can fix that." He reached for her shirt.

She leaned back and wrapped her arms around her waist. "No, we can't. Look, this was unbelievable, but it shouldn't have happened."

Didn't she think he knew that? Hell, all he'd come around looking for was a kiss. Not a sexual encounter just this side of sinful. Or maybe *that* side of it. "I know."

"And it can't happen again."

For a second, he thought he'd misheard. Because after what they'd shared a moment ago, he couldn't imagine she was any less anxious than he to find out what they could make each other feel without any clothes at all. In a bed. All night long.

"You wanna run that by me again?"

"I'm not in the market for a lover, Spence," she said.

"My life is changing and I'm trying to change with it." The resolute stiffness of her jaw told him she meant business.

"You going into a convent after you close Temptation?"

A sound that was half laugh, half groan escaped her lips. "If I did, I'd have to buy stock in a vibrator company."

A sexy vision shot right through his brain.

"But no," she continued before he could interrupt, "I'm not giving up sex completely. I'm trying to…change my focus. My direction. My choices."

He wasn't sure what she was getting at, but he could tell by the stiff way she held her body that she meant what she said. Cat wasn't in the market for a relationship, even a purely sexual one. She was putting up barriers and, judging by the mournful look in her eyes, they were as difficult for her as they were for him. But she obviously trusted him to respect her wishes because she hadn't walked out in search of more clothes.

"All right, Cat," he murmured, "I understand. I'll give you your space." He stepped back, creating more distance—physically and mentally—between them. "We both need to get downstairs and get to work, anyway."

He'd said what she wanted to hear, but a tiny frown appeared on Cat's brow. Dylan hid a grin, more sure than ever that she didn't *really* want him to back off.

Of course, he'd never *really* intended to.

He'd been sincere…he'd leave now, not push the issue, not force her to act on the attraction so hot between them it could melt glass. Yeah, he'd definitely back off.

But only until he could get her to admit she didn't mean it.

5

By Sunday night, Cat was sure her plans to be responsible, respectable and, well, *good*, were gonna go up in a ball of flames. Flames sparked by a hundred-and-seventy pounds of walking sin named Spence, who'd literally had her in the palm of his hand less than twenty-four hours ago.

And who was, right now, at this moment, making verbal love to about fifty other women.

"Oh, my, would I love to have one hour alone with that man."

Cat didn't have to look up to know the redhead who'd made the comment was staring wide-eyed at the guy playing bass guitar on the small stage in Temptation. Every woman here was thinking the same thing. Of one hour. Or one night. With *him*.

"I'm soooo glad I heard about this," the woman continued. "To think that otherwise, I'd have been at Bible study tonight!"

"I'm sure God'll understand," Cat muttered, not even trying to hide her sarcasm.

Sarcasm obviously wasn't enough to pierce the lust in the redhead's brain. She nodded in pious agreement.

Cat stared around the room at the dozens of other drones looking just as slack-jawed as this one. Word had spread after Friday's and Saturday's performances, and there had actually been a line at the door by 7:00 p.m. tonight. They were packed, wall to wall, for the first time in months. There were enough women in this place to stock a Mary Kay convention. And she'd lay even money there were a number of females here who'd arrived alone...but didn't want to *leave* alone.

Something deep inside her clenched. If he left with another woman, she was going to get violent. Man, that was hard to admit, even to herself, because it obviously proved she was already hopelessly out of her depth with a guy she'd sworn she couldn't have. Well, couldn't have any more than she'd already *had* him.

"Here's your drink," she said as she swirled a stir stick in the redhead's gin and tonic—heavy on the tonic, because if the woman had too much more alcohol, she'd be diving onto the stage.

To Cat's surprise, as she slid the glass across the sticky surface of the pitted bar, some of the drink sloshed out. That was when she realized her fingers were shaky, as was her whole body. Shaky. Tense. Aware. She'd been all of those things since *he'd* walked through the door forty-eight hours ago.

Man, she needed to get laid. By him.

No. That's the old Cat, she reminded herself. The new one wasn't ruled by her sex drive, her empty pocketbook or her love of adventure. Even if it was nice to occasionally wonder...*what if?* Which she'd been doing a lot after the incredible way he'd made her feel, using only his hand and his mouth. Not to mention his seductive voice whispering erotic things in her ear.

She closed her eyes and sighed at the memory.

What if Dinah hadn't knocked? What if she'd fallen earlier and they'd had more time alone? What if he'd forgotten his keys again last night and come back inside, like he had on Friday? Would she have had the strength to keep her barriers in place?

Probably not.

The fantasies of what could have happened after her barriers crumbled had filled her thoughts all night and all day.

"I need two Sour Apple Martinis and two bottles of Bud," said Vicki, an old friend of Cat's who'd come in to help out tonight. "And maybe a side of band member to go with it."

Cat gave her a look through half-lowered lashes. "Oh?"

Sighing, Vicki said, "I'd love to have a musician sandwich."

"As long as it's a blond musician sandwich," she snapped back, before thinking better of the words.

Vicki's eyes nearly popped out of her head. "Whoa, girl, you got a claim on one of the dark-haired ones?"

Wishing she'd kept her big, fat mouth shut, Cat stepped away from Vicki's curious gaze and busied herself making the drinks. "Never mind," she said as she put them on the waitress's tray.

Vicki merely smirked, having known her long enough to know when Cat was infatuated with a man. "Is it the piano player or the long-haired hunk with the bass guitar?"

"Whadda you think?"

"Bass player," Vicki replied without hesitation. "He's incredibly hot. And he seems familiar for some reason." Staring across the room, she sighed. "Must be the movie-star looks."

After Vicki walked away, Cat quickly got caught up with the other orders, barely hearing the music. When things did slow down for a second, she paused to listen, recognizing an old song. The low note of Spence's bass guitar thrummed in her chest, and the way he growled the words to "Bad To The Bone" made her—and every other woman here—want to find out just how bad he could be.

Very bad. But oh, so incredibly *good*.

She still couldn't get their crazy-wild encounter in her kitchen out of her mind. Whenever she licked her lips she still tasted him there. The way he practically made love to the microphone while singing hot, pulsing, headboard-slamming music sure wasn't helping her forget.

And when the song changed again and Spence invited every woman in the place to light his fire, she was ready to go all teenage-girl-at-her-first-concert on him and start throwing underwear at his feet. Teeny-tiny underwear. Like the ones that had inspired such a powerful reaction in him last night.

"Cat, did you hear me? The phone's ringing!"

Cat finally shook off the warm, lethargic lust and looked at Dinah, who'd obviously been trying to get her attention. Then she turned to the phone, spying the number on the caller ID.

Laine. Calling for her expected "don't screw this up" chat. Cat was in no mood to hear it. Dammit, if her sister was so sure she was going to louse things up, why had she run out on her when Cat had needed her the most? As far as Cat was concerned, Laine had waived all rights to any say in what happened the minute she'd walked out the door without a second thought for the loss of their family's heritage.

She yanked the receiver to her ear. "Temptation."

"Cat?"

"Lainey?" she replied through clenched teeth, knowing the nickname drove her sister nuts.

"Have you called the auction house yet? We need to get some cash for the furniture to pay off the liquor supplier."

Gee, nothing like a little small talk to get the conversation rolling. She couldn't help replying, "Hi, sister dear, how are you? How was your day? I'm sure it's *so* difficult dealing with everything *all on your own* since I left you there without a thought at all for *anybody but myself.*"

"Please don't start, Cat," Laine replied. "You'll be fine. Just follow my list."

Her list. The stupid list. The one that might as well have started with, "Cat, you're useless, so here, I'll save you yet again by telling you every single thing to do."

"What list?" Cat said, wondering if the pounding in her head was caused by the music or by the stress of always playing this role in the Sheehan family. God, sometimes she got so bloody tired of being either the screwup or the bitch.

"The one I taped to the bar that explained step-by-step what you needed to do this week." Laine's impatient sigh was nearly inaudible. Nearly.

Cat rubbed at the corners of her eyes, wondering why it was so hard to tell her sister how she felt. To open up and change the boundaries of their relationship. Laine was warm and smart and wonderful. She would listen, of course she would.

But deep in her heart, Cat knew the truth. Laine might listen. But she wouldn't *hear*. So she responded in Catlike fashion, in words Laine *would* understand. And expect. "Oh, I wondered what that was. Some guy spilled whiskey all over it Friday night. I threw it away."

A pregnant pause followed and Cat almost regretted the lie. Nobody had spilled whiskey on Laine's damn list. Cat had balled it up and thrown it in the trash the day her sister had left. If everybody else felt free to leave her alone to deal with closing down Temptation, then she was gonna do it *her* way.

"I'll e-mail you another copy. And call the auction house first thing tomorrow."

She shook her head. Same old Laine, who'd never believe Cat had called the auction house Thursday. She'd been to the bank. She'd ordered enough stock to get them through the month. She'd contacted movers. She'd called for an application for college, deciding maybe it wasn't so crazy to think she could get a degree and pursue her secret dream of becoming a high school teacher.

Few people knew that dream, which was exactly the way Cat liked it. She didn't want to be laughed at, which, she figured, was exactly the reaction she'd get from most people.

After all, she was nothing like her sister. Laine had been the valedictorian of her senior class.

Cat had been the Girl Most Likely To Meet Hugh Hefner.

"Cat, did you hear me? What have you been doing since I left?"

Oh, nothing much. She'd just handled everything at the bar, looked in the want ads for a job and the apartment guide for a place to live. All on her little lonesome. Imagine that. She'd even had something approaching a sexual interlude with the most attractive man she'd ever known. None of which she could tell her sister. "I'm busy," she finally said, too tired to continue these dramatic family games.

"Please, Cat. We have to get moving on these things."

As if Laine cared. There was no *we* in Temptation anymore. There was only Cat. "Yeah, sure, *we* do."

Oh, Lord, her voice had broken a bit on the word *we*. She missed her sister. Missed Tess. Missed Gracie, who'd been so distracted all weekend. How, when she was surrounded by so many people, could she still feel so lonely?

She'd never felt more so, not until now, this moment,

when she thought—truly thought—about everything she had to do in the coming weeks. Selling her memories piece by piece. Saying goodbye to things that had been so precious to her. Packing up every part of her life and trying to figure out where to go from here.

Alone. Entirely alone.

Then she raised her eyes and looked at the stage. From across the expanse of the room, Spence met her stare. A frown tugged at his brow, and he tilted his head to the side, silently asking her if she was okay. And suddenly, though he'd been a stranger to her two days before, Cat again began to acknowledge those unusual feelings she'd had since the moment they'd met.

That as long as Spence was around, she was never going to feel alone again.

BY THE END of the final set Sunday night, Dylan had begun to realize he had a problem. A big one. There was a real flaw with his plan to convince Cat to change her mind about letting something happen between them: after tonight, he wouldn't have any legitimate reason to see her again.

Well, no reason he could tell *her*. In truth, he had dozens of reasons—like the whole suspecting-he-needed-to-see-her-face-in-order-to-want-to-keep-breathing bit—but that seemed a bit much. Particularly since she still assumed him to be a stranger, which was the other sticky point. He hadn't come clean with her yet…hadn't even told her his full name. He debated on whether to just walk up to the bar during a break, start flirting, and challenge her to remember where they'd met before.

She'd be interested at first, her eyes would sparkle as he dared her to guess, taunting her about their shared past. Then, when she finally figured it out—or when he finally told her—that merry sparkle would fade, to be replaced by the friendly-but-uninterested look she'd always bestowed on him in the old days.

You jackass, you're nothing like you were in the old days.

And he wasn't, certainly not in appearance, and definitely not in attitude or self-confidence. But the same old sensible, introspective brainiac lurked beneath his rocker surface. And he wasn't sure Cat would like that guy, much less want him to put his hand where Dylan's had been the night before.

He closed his eyes and threw his head back, relishing the memory as he backed up Josh's version of a Stones classic. The feel of her drenching his fingers, the taste of her mouth, the coos she'd made as she came, the rich smell of her warm body.

He was getting turned on all over again just remembering it.

"Whoa," someone called.

He glanced over and saw Banks, watching him. "You *got* some."

Dylan shot him a withering glare.

"Or you're thinking about getting some," Banks said, his yell barely audible over the sound of the music.

But somebody obviously heard him, because a few of the women at a table closest to the stage began to whoop and holler. "I'll give you something, baby," one of them screamed.

And she did. Her shirt. With a suddenness that caught him completely off guard, the woman whipped off her top and flung it toward the stage. It came flying at him and landed on his head.

Dylan shook it off, catching it in his hands. Then, because the lights were damn hot and he was damn mad at both the woman and Banks, he used the T-shirt to wipe the sweat off his face and neck. Throwing it into a corner, he kept right on playing.

The women in the crowd went nuts. "Take mine," one yelled.

"Hell," he murmured, watching as several inebriated-looking females stood on their chairs or beside their tables and reached for their waistbands or their buttons.

But before another shirt went flying, a blond figure erupted into his field of vision. Cat leapt up onto the stage, pointing out at the audience. Dylan and his bandmates instinctively brought the music down a notch in volume. "Next woman who removes one piece of her clothes gets thrown out," she yelled. "And possibly arrested."

A few groans greeted Cat's announcement, but she ignored them. She did, however, cast one withering glance at Dylan, her expression fierce and her green eyes snapping with anger.

Jumping back down, she beelined toward the bar, never even looking back. Which was good. Because that meant she didn't see the cocky grin Dylan couldn't keep from his face.

That hadn't been a concerned business owner trying to keep things from getting out of hand in her establishment. That had been a jealous woman who'd been lying through her teeth when she'd claimed she didn't want to be involved with him.

And suddenly, though he still wasn't sure how he was going to make sure he got to stick around, he began to feel better.

When they ended the song—which had been their fifth encore—Banks immediately rose from his keyboard, signaling the definite end of the show to the crowd. He practically danced his way across the stage, his amusement visible in his smile. "You got her, man. She is yours. I thought she was going to go after the brunette who threw the shirt and snatch her bald."

Dylan lowered his guitar. "Shut up, Banks. Don't think I'll forget you caused that incident. And you're as full of it about her as you are about everything else."

Banks, impossible to insult as always, almost bounced on his toes. "Talk about avenging goddess. She must have a total case. I think she threw a beer at someone to get over here before any more women started stripping in your general direction."

"Doesn't matter," Dylan muttered as he turned toward the back of the stage and reached for a bottle of water. He drew deeply from it, needing the fluid on his dry vocal cords. After draining what was left inside, he crumpled the plastic bottle in his hand and two-pointed it into an empty box in the corner. "She says she's too busy shutting this place down to get involved with anyone, so there's no point in even trying. After tonight, I have no more excuses to see her."

Josh and Jeremy walked over, having extricated themselves from the fans who'd crowded around the foot of the stage. Jeremy grabbed Dylan's shoulder. "Man, what did you do to piss off the bartender? She looked like she was gonna rip you a new one."

Josh shook his head, grinning at his brother's naiveté. "Obviously our friend Spence here has been making a little extra time with the Cat woman. It's like a live version of *Revenge of the Nerds*."

Dylan glared at Banks, who had the grace to avert his stare in guilt, the loudmouth.

Jeremy's eyes jaw dropped. "You and the blonde? Man, I've been staring at her for three days, waiting to make my move."

Dylan's eyes narrowed. "Don't even think about it."

The kid put his hands up, palms out. "No sweat, I'm backing off. She probably wouldn't have been interested anyway. She carded me and knows how old I am."

Josh punched his brother in the shoulder. "You tried to buy beer? Dammit, bro, that was part of the deal with us letting you replace Charlie. That you'd play by the rules. All of them."

"Busted," Banks muttered as Jeremy stammered to explain.

God, had he ever been as young as Jeremy? At nineteen, Dylan had been a senior in college. And now, six years later, he felt positively ancient compared to the young drummer. Maybe because his parents and teachers had been treating him like an adult since the age when most kids were just hitting puberty.

By unspoken agreement, the four of them began packing up their gear as the crowd drifted out of the bar, though a few women did try to stick around to offer phone numbers to anyone who would take them. Cat would have none of that. She practically shooed the stragglers out with her broom, reminding any complainers of the town ordinance against bars staying open past midnight on Sunday.

"One of these days, we're gonna be successful enough to have roadies to do this crap," Jeremy said as he went through the routine of disassembling his drum set.

Dylan doubted it, mainly because he had no interest in going further. But maybe Jeremy would. The kid was more serious about his music than the rest of them ever had been.

The Four G's had been formed in college, when he and Banks had hooked up with Josh and their former drummer, Charlie Moss. They'd had a lot in common—all young college freshmen, Dylan being the youngest. They'd all been studious and smart, they'd all been rock fanatics. Most of all, they'd all been geeks.

Hence their name. The Four G's.

Jeremy still didn't know the full story behind the name. He'd once said he figured it had something to do with their last names, Josh being a Garrity and all. That Banks, Spencer and Moss didn't start with a G hadn't seemed to occur to him. And they hadn't enlightened the teen—because Jeremy probably would have taken offense at the label.

"Well, until those glorious roadie days, every man gets to handle his own *instrument*," Banks said to no one in particular. Then he snickered, amused by his own off-color wit.

Dylan kept his attention on his work, not daring to look in Cat's direction while she wiped down tables with the two waitresses. And he definitely didn't try to talk to her—not while Banks and the other guys were here. The last thing he wanted was one of them stepping in to try to "help" him by telling Cat tonight's incident was nothing to get upset about.

With his luck, they'd make some comment about the girl who'd leapt on him after a performance at a fair in Tremont last month. Or the one who stowed away in his car last winter. Not to mention the one he'd almost had to get a restraining order against. Those incidents were almost enough to make him rethink this whole band thing and just stay quietly in his house, doing the independent software consulting work that was his day job.

Lost in his own thoughts, he hardly even noticed that Banks had disappeared. Casting a quick glance around, he saw his friend at the bar, chatting up the young waitress. And Cat.

"I'll kill him." Hopping off the stage, he strode over to join them. If Banks had told Cat the truth about Dylan's identity, he wasn't going to be responsible for his own actions.

"Hey, man, I was just telling Miss Sheehan how much we appreciate the gig," Banks said, sounding way too innocent for the prank-playing fiend Dylan knew him to be.

"We do appreciate it," Dylan murmured.

"You guys were great," the dark-haired waitress said. Then she peered more closely at Dylan. "Do I know you from somewhere?"

"Spence is famous," Banks said, stepping between them. "Women are always tossing their clothes at him."

Dead friend walking. That was Billy Banks.

Banks looked at Cat and gave her one of those boyish innocent looks that had fooled so many of his competitors back on the political debate team. "It's not his fault, Miss Sheehan. I made a comment that got that woman riled up earlier. Not Dylan."

Cat's gave him a triumphant look. "*Dylan*, huh?"

She knew his name. Dylan's fingers clenched into fists at his sides as he waited, watching for a spark of recognition, a hint of curiosity, or understanding. Instead, she pursed her lip and asked, "First or last?"

"Huh?"

"Which is your first name and which is your last?"

"Dylan's my first name," he said through a tight jaw and an unexpected thickness in his throat.

Still nothing. No widening of the eyes, no puzzlement on her brow. Certainly no *Aha!* His name meant absolutely nothing to her. Which shouldn't have ticked him off. But it did.

"Seriously," Banks said, still playing some kind of weird matchmaking game, "it wasn't his fault. It was mine."

Cat's shrug was a bit *too* casual. "Not a problem. I just didn't want it to go any further. I plan for Temptation to finish out her run in style. Not with a raid."

"So you're really closing?" Banks asked.

Cat nodded, her jaw tightening. "We have two more weeks. Then it's *sayonara*."

Dylan watched for the pain and sure enough, it flashed in her eyes. Cat was no closer to accepting the reality of this loss now than she had been Friday night. In fact, she looked even more bereft. More tired, world-weary. His flash of anger that he'd been so utterly forgettable dissipated, replaced by a strange ache he couldn't contain.

He didn't like to see her hurting. Didn't like to think of her alone in this place, watching it being torn apart piece by piece as she wondered where she'd go and what she'd do. He'd really like to know where the hell her family was, because he had some things he'd like to say to them about dumping the responsibility for this mess right onto her slim shoulders.

"Speaking of *sayonara*, I'm outta here," Vicki said, grabbing her purse and shoving a handful of cash from her apron pocket into it. "Thanks for the work—great tips tonight!"

"Thank *you*," Cat replied. "We couldn't have managed without you and I really do appreciate it."

Dinah echoed her. "You're a lifesaver, hon. Come on, me 'n' Zeke'll walk you to your car."

The women disappeared into the kitchen to leave through the rear exit. Once they were gone, Banks sat at one of the stools at the bar and stared at Cat. "Well," he said, "I hope you continue to have a lot of help. Looks like there's stuff to be done around here. You could get some real money for some of those antique signs, the mugs, the posters and the old-fashioned jukebox. Not to mention the light fixtures—is that handblown glass?"

Cat glanced around in disinterest. "Yeah." Then she ran a weary hand through her long hair, her fingertips rubbing lightly on her temple, as if easing away an ache. "It's going to be a long couple of weeks with tons to do." Shaking her head, she muttered something under her breath. Something that sounded like "Thanks again, Laine."

"Well, if you need any help, Spence is very handy to have around. And he could use the work. Playing in a bar band doesn't exactly bring home the bacon." Banks managed to keep a straight face as he held a palm up to keep Dylan from interrupting. "Hey, bud, I know you're embarrassed, but everybody's been down on their luck. It's just too bad you can't live in your car this time since you unloaded it for that crotch rocket."

Dylan's jaw dropped. "What..."

"Jeez," Banks continued, embellishing his outlandish story for Cat's benefit. "He's a wild man on his Harley."

Dylan merely grunted in disbelief.

"Starving musicians, we all do what we can," Banks added, sounding so ridiculous Dylan expected Cat to burst into laughter at any moment. She couldn't possibly believe any of this.

"Shut the hell up, Billy."

His friend ignored him. "I'd give him a place to stay, but I'm crashing with a buddy in Tremont." He gave Dylan an evil grin. "He's got a great house, with a pool...but it's full."

Dylan's house. He was talking about Dylan's house!

"And Josh and Jeremy live with their parents," Banks continued, "so that's no good."

Cat, whose brow had furrowed during Banks's ridiculous lies, turned to Dylan. "You really have no place to go?"

"He's full of crap," Dylan said. "The motorcycle..."

"Isn't running well, I know," Banks said. "You'll be lucky if it doesn't break down on you again tonight."

Motorcycle. As if Dylan would ever sit on Jeremy's

deathmobile when it was turned off. Much less ride it on the street! And Banks damn well knew it.

Dylan didn't know what to do first—tell Cat the truth or just beat his *former* best friend to a bloody pulp. Particularly since Cat was now staring hard at him, eyes narrowed and her head tilted as if she were deep in thought. "Is that so?" she asked.

Wondering why her voice had trembled a bit, Dylan immediately retorted. "No, it's not."

Banks shook his head sadly. "He's a proud one, all right."

Clenching his back teeth, Dylan prepared to make his friend eat either his words or Dylan's fist, but when Cat delicately cleared her throat, he paused.

"Well," she said, drawing the word out as she nibbled on the corner of her nicely healed bottom lip, "I hate to admit it, but I *could* use some help around here."

Dylan froze, the heated denial of Banks's story dying on his lips. Meeting her stare, he looked for any hidden meaning, any secret agenda, but saw nothing. Not until a slow flush of color rose in her cheeks as she correctly interpreted what he'd been silently asking: Did she *really* need help? Or had she changed her mind about wanting a lover?

Not even waiting for his reply, Cat suddenly busied herself drying some glasses, turning slightly away so he couldn't figure out what was going on in her pretty head.

"You wanna explain that?"

"I don't want charity," she said, her voice as stiff as her shoulders. Then she added, "And I'm not offering it, either."

"What *are* you offering?" His voice held a challenge.

She put the glass away and finally turned back to look him in the eye. A pregnant pause made him wonder if she was making some big decision, or just being careful with her words. "A job. If you really need one, I *could* use the help."

"Cat…"

"He does," Banks announced, clapping his hand flat on the surface of the bar. The grin on the guy's face was positively gleeful. Hopping off his stool, Banks added, "I'll let you guys work it out." Then he turned and walked over to the stage, immediately engaging in a lively conversation with Jeremy.

If it had anything to do with the damn Harley parked outside, Dylan was gonna lose it.

But he couldn't think too much about that. Because Cat was still standing behind the bar, a few feet away, suddenly appearing so small and delicate. She looked around the room, shaking her head a bit as if overwhelmed by what she saw.

"Are you okay?" he asked, wondering how serious she was about needing help. She hadn't mentioned it before. Then again, he didn't remember Cat as the type who'd ever ask for help, unless she was truly at the end of her rope.

"I hadn't figured out how I was going to get the fixtures down or get some stuff out of the attic. I guess it hadn't really sunk in until tonight that I have to do all this by myself."

"I do want to help you," Dylan murmured, wondering how to offer to stick around while at the same time disabusing her of the notion that he was an unemployed loser looking for a handout.

She wrapped her arms around her body, rubbing her hands up and down on her skin, as if suddenly cold. "I can't pay you too much, but maybe this could work out for both of us. I know you'd be saving me money. If I have to have the broker do all the work as well as finding the buyers and handling the sales, I won't make nearly as much."

"You don't have to pay me…"

She immediately dropped her arms to her side, her chin

lifting a notch. "Like I said, I'm not looking for charity. If you want a job, I can give you one, short-term." Faint color rose in her cheeks for some reason. When she continued, he began to understand why. "And I can even offer you a place to crash. There's a small storage room in the back, with a cot and bathroom. You can eat whatever you care to fix in the kitchen and I'll pay you what I can."

Stay here. Under the same roof. While she slept upstairs. If he'd ever had any willpower where Cat Sheehan was concerned, he knew it wouldn't last through the first night.

He wondered if *hers* would.

"Well, what do you think?"

Dylan didn't know what to say. He simply watched her, absorbing her words, but paying even closer attention to her body language. That weariness he'd noticed earlier was back, evident in the tiny furrow on her brow and the slowness of her movements. The slight tremble in her hand as she wiped off the bar told him even more. She was tired, overwhelmed and in over her head.

But there was something else…a faint gleam in her glistening green eyes. A hint of suppressed excitement in the tense position of her body. A sense of expectation in the deep breaths she took in, then slowly released.

Something else was going on, he knew it as sure as he knew the lyrics to every Aerosmith song ever recorded. Cat had more on her mind than offering him a job. But Dylan didn't trust himself to speculate on what.

"He's a con artist, Cat," he said, making one more effort to get things out in the open. "Banks manipulated you into this."

Cat didn't flinch, didn't back down or rescind her offer. Instead, she said, "No, he didn't. I'm not easily manipulated." She leaned across the bar, lowering her voice though no one stood within a dozen feet of them. Licking her lips, she whispered, "I don't want to do this alone, Spence. Will you stay? Please?"

Oh, God. Would he stay? Of course he wanted to, not only so he could spend more time with her, but also because she needed help. Cat truly needed someone to lean on—she was admitting it aloud, for possibly the first time in her life.

And she wanted him to be that someone. At least, the him she *thought* he was—Spence, the broke, unemployed, homeless musician.

If he told her the truth—that he wasn't some down-on-his-luck guitar player—she'd change her mind. He knew it. Cat was too proud to take charity and she'd feel like a fool for ever mentioning it. She'd put up a wall and retreat behind it and he'd be walking out the door.

If he kept his mouth shut, he'd be silently agreeing with all the bullshit Banks had been spewing a few minutes ago.

But he'd be staying.

Dylan didn't want to continue the lie. Now that she knew his name, part of him actually wanted the truth to come out, once and for all. Still, he couldn't risk her refusing his help, couldn't let Cat shoulder the burden her family had seen fit to thrust on her. Most important, he couldn't leave here with so many questions still unanswered between them.

How could he let Cat push him back out of her life before the two of them took a shot at figuring out how he might eventually fit into it?

"Dylan?"

That cinched it. The way his first name sounded on her lips nearly made him shake.

So be it.

He was damned if he told her the truth and damned if he didn't. So if he had to be damned, he was gonna do it right here with the woman he'd wanted for nearly a decade. And let the chips fall where they may.

"Okay, Cat," he murmured, his voice low and unwavering. "I'll stay."

6

CAT HAD MADE THE DECISION to seduce Spence about one minute after she'd learned he was unemployed and a drifter.

Soon. Immediately. *Tonight.*

Actually, she'd been toying with the idea from the moment she'd hung up the phone with Laine earlier and had met Spence's stare across the crowded bar. Something had happened—something electrifying and emotional and completely unexpected. She wasn't sure why, but she hadn't been able to shake the feeling that this *thing* building between them had been destined to happen. In that moment, it had risen above the sexual want they'd been dancing around since Friday night and had suddenly become…more.

Thank heaven she hadn't told anybody else about her new plans for herself and her life, because they'd think her crazy, given this decision. The truth about Spence's situation might have made her run screaming in the opposite direction *if* she'd already succeeded in her transformation from the reckless Cat to the mature, responsible one.

Right. It hadn't happened yet. Because, in all honesty, she'd set out a list of nearly impossible goals. How she'd ever thought she could deal with losing the business, as well as completely overhauling her personal life, she had no idea.

A girl couldn't take on too much at once, right? Saying goodbye to her family heritage was quite enough all by itself, without throwing virtual celibacy into the mix. Sure, she would still do both, only she'd do them one at a time. After the bar closed for good, she could become the new, responsible, non-bad-boy-loving Catherine Sheehan.

Not now. For now she was going to enjoy the hell out of Temptation…and *temptation*. With a man who epitomized the word.

"One last fling," she mumbled as she replaced the last of the clean bar glasses and glanced across the room. The tall, lean man standing there winding up cable was the perfect candidate for a fling. He was laid-back and unencumbered. Probably unreliable, not to mention unpredictable. A guy like Spence was as likely to be gone tomorrow as to still be here. Which meant he'd expect nothing, demand nothing and want nothing in return.

Her heart wouldn't be in danger, as it would have been if there were a chance of something real developing between them. Like if he had a job, a home, roots that tied him to this place, which might mean he could settle down and build a future with a woman.

If he'd been *that* guy, she'd have shoved him out the door, figuring it was better to avoid the chance of heartbreak altogether. But he wasn't that guy, and she could go into this with her eyes wide-open and her heart tightly guarded.

With no chance of getting hurt.

Over the next half hour, Cat finished cleaning up the bar, watching as Spence and his bandmates loaded up their instruments and carried everything out to the parking lot. She noticed the curious, somewhat salacious looks Spence received from the others. To give him credit, he did not acknowledge them in any way or act the least bit cocky about staying when they were all leaving.

Because he wasn't sure *why* he was staying. Not really. He didn't know if she'd asked him to remain here because she needed him. Or because she wanted him.

Both. She did want him, had wanted him desperately since the moment she'd laid eyes on him Friday night. But she also needed help, and he needed a job. It seemed like a perfect solution. She'd have someone to help her close down the bar and get this need for one last wild, reckless fling out of her system. He'd have employment and a place to crash for a couple of weeks.

Then he'd go on his merry way. On to his next town, his next bar. *His next woman?*

Thrusting the thought away, Cat refused to acknowledge the flash of dismay that accompanied it. She had no business worrying about what Spence might do after he left here. Because if she did, that would mean she cared about him.

Impossible. Reverting to the reckless Cat who'd indulge in a passionate affair was all about Temptation and a need for release. Not about genuine emotion and vulnerability. Definitely not about love. She wouldn't allow that, not when she knew damn well he could break her heart when he left. As he inevitably would. After all, didn't everyone?

"G'night, Cat," one of the musicians called. It had been one of the blond ones—the young drummer who'd tried to buy beer. "I'll come back to visit before you close down."

"I'll have the ginger ale all ready for you," Cat replied, grinning as he rolled his eyes.

And soon, so soon she didn't have a chance to prepare

mentally—much less physically—she and Spence were alone. Locking the door behind his friends, he slowly turned to face her across the deserted room.

She shivered, just a bit. From nervousness or anticipation, she really couldn't tell. Nor did she care, since they both simply heightened the delicious tension.

"Considering the crowds in here this weekend," he said, filling the silence, "have you thought about relocating?"

Cat shrugged. "It's crossed my mind." Then she ran her hand across the surface of the bar, so smooth and warm—almost living—beneath her touch. "But it wouldn't be the same. What mattered was the place. This particular building."

He nodded, instantly understanding. Then he reached for the light switches beside the front door and flipped them down. The room descended into that red semidarkness, only the overhead, colored glass lamps remaining on.

Holding her breath, Cat waited, wondering if Spence had already realized what was on her mind. When he slowly reached toward the cord for the blinds covering the front windows, she suspected he did. Because with one easy pull of the cord, he shut out the view from the street. Shut out the rest of the world.

"Thanks," she murmured.

He didn't answer. He merely waited for her next move. So she made it. "Have I thanked you for walking through my door Friday night?" Licking her lips, she added, "And have I told you how glad I am that you're staying...with me?"

That seemed to be enough. He gave her one tiny nod of understanding and she waited for him to approach. Instead, he surprised her by walking over to the old jukebox near the stage. Something of a family heirloom, the jukebox was original to the bar, right down to the music it contained. After her grandparents had died, the rest of the family had decided to leave the records exactly as they were, reflecting that generation's taste in music.

The old standards didn't appeal to their new, younger clientele, so the machine seldom got used. Especially not with the shiny new karaoke machine in the opposite corner. But the jukebox did work, as Spence seemed to know. Glancing over the song list, he inserted several quarters into the slot and pressed a few of the numbered buttons. In the thick silence of the room, he turned around to look at her, the intensity of his expression saying more than words ever could.

The whir of the machinery and the click of the record falling were only slightly more audible than the beating of Cat's heart. When the sultry strains of an old jazz tune emerged from the old, tinny speakers, she closed her eyes, letting the seductive quality of the music fill her head.

She sensed the moment Spence reached her side, though he'd moved with catlike silence across the room. She hadn't had to look to know he was there. Feeling his warmth, she breathed deeply to inhale his male scent. Her whole body arched a bit closer to him, drawn by his warmth. His presence.

When she opened her eyes, she saw him watching her with visible hunger. "Slow and smoky enough?" he whispered.

Immediately knowing what he meant, she nodded. Without another word, she kicked off her sneakers, then reached for his hand. His fingers tightened reflexively around hers for a split second before he helped her onto the step stool she kept for reaching bottles on the top shelf. She stepped up, then up again, until, with his help, she ascended onto the bar.

Within a heartbeat, he joined her there. "Dance with me?"

Feeling the thrum of the music—not to mention a bone-deep, sensually inspired lethargy—Cat nodded and stepped into his arms. And was utterly lost. Lost to everything else but this time and this place and this man.

Their bodies fit together as if they had been made for one another, the soft curves of hers mating perfectly with the hard breadth of his. She'd been incredibly intimate with Spence in some ways, but had never been held this closely by him. The contact was both electric and erotic. She felt it from head to toe.

"Careful now," he said softly, beginning to sway to the music, still holding her tight.

"You won't let me fall," she replied, meaning much more than physically falling off the bar.

Bathed in the reddish glow of the overhead light, his eyes glittered as he replied, "No, Cat, I won't let you fall."

Then they were silent. Cat tucked her head against his neck, resting it on his shoulder. Her lips brushed his skin and she couldn't resist sampling his salty taste with one gentle swipe of her tongue. He reacted with a hiss, nothing more.

Inhaling his earthy, spicy scent, she completely relaxed and gave herself over to the music, instinctively following his every move. She should have known he would be able to dance, since he moved, breathed and thought in rhythm.

What she couldn't have imagined was that slow dancing with Spence would be like making love. Sweet, hungry, erotic love.

"I like this music," he murmured.

"It's not exactly AC/DC."

He laughed softly. "It'll do."

Yeah. It would do.

With one hand curled over her hip, he used the other to lazily stroke the small of her back. His fingers dipped low, sliding beneath the waistband of her jeans. When he began tracing small circles there, Cat knew he was picturing her tattoo, following the swirling pattern with his touch. The wicked images he'd spoken about in her apartment the previous evening made her shiver with anticipation.

"You're not cold are you?"

She shook her head, saying nothing, not having the energy to form words in her brain, much less speak them. She had only the energy to keep moving her feet, to keep shifting her thighs against his, to keep feeling the incredible delight of her breasts rubbing against his mile-wide chest.

The record ended but they didn't stop moving. Soon enough there was another whir, another click and the strains of another song banishing the silence. This one was just as slow, just as smoky.

So was her whisper. "Kiss me, Spence."

He complied, dipping down to catch her mouth with his, parting his lips and allowing their tongues to meet and dance, as well. He tasted delicious—hot and sweet—and Cat tilted her head, kissing him back with lazy, lethargic lust.

Without giving it any thought, Cat reached for the waist of his jeans and tugged his T-shirt free. She slid it up, her palms gliding over his taut skin every inch of the way. He was warm and firm, his body a little slick from his performance on stage, and the heat of the night. Not to mention their dance.

Cat couldn't resist running her hands over his chest, scraping the tips of her nails lightly across his flat nipples, rubbing at the flexing sinews of muscle on his shoulder. The man's body was to die for—hard and ripped and hot all over.

Reaching for the bottom of her shirt, Spence equaled

things out a bit, pulling it off her with the same deliberation Cat had used. His fingertips danced across every bit
of her skin as it was revealed.

"Mmm," she moaned, unable to manage anything else
except the deep, throaty sound of pleasure at the warmth
of his touch.

Echoing it, he reached around and deftly unfastened her
bra, pushing each strap off her shoulders. Cat shrugged
and the flimsy fabric fell to join their shirts, then she
pressed against him again so they could dance topless.

The feel of his chest rubbing at the tips of her breasts
through their clothes had been incredibly pleasurable.

This was mind-blowing.

"You're beautiful," he murmured. Raising a hand, he
cupped her breast, tweaking her nipple with delicate
flicks of his fingers until Cat was ready to beg for more.
Like his mouth.

He seemed to read her mind. "I want to taste you."

Answering with her body, she leaned back and offered
herself to him. He nibbled his way down her neck, pausing to lick the tiny hollow beneath her collarbone. She
whimpered as he moved lower, until he was kissing the
top curve of her breast. And when he slid his tongue farther to delicately lick at her hard and sensitive nipple, she
cried out incoherently.

"You taste as good as you look," he mumbled before
closing his mouth entirely over the tip of her breast and
sucking deep.

Thankfully, Spence still had an arm around her waist
because Cat's legs began to shake. "I've got you," he
whispered.

Somewhere far away, there was brief silence, then another click and another song began. This one with a

stronger, more driving beat that seemed to echo the rising tempo, the heat building ever higher between them.

Lowering her to the top of the bar, Spence knelt in front of her, still doing crazy, heavenly things with his mouth and his magical hands. Leaving her reclining there, he hopped down to the floor and stood before her. He leaned down, continuing his hungry exploration of her breasts, her midriff and her stomach.

When he reached for the snap of her jeans, Cat moaned again. "I want you so much."

"Ditto."

"I don't know if I can even walk long enough to go upstairs to my place," she whispered, unable to bear the thought of even a brief interruption.

He took hold of her hips and tugged her toward him, until she was sitting on the edge of the bar, her legs dangling over the sides. "We're not going anywhere," he said. "I'm can't wait one more minute for this. I've wanted you for too long."

Even more inflamed by the raw power of his desire— as if he'd hungered for her for years instead of mere days— Cat arched back. Lifting her hips, she watched as he unfastened her jeans and tugged them down.

"Cat, I've dreamed of this, of having you," he murmured as he looked his fill at her. "You're more beautiful than I ever imagined."

Bathed in the soft light, and in the heat of his eyes, Cat *felt* beautiful. Powerful. Irresistible. Like a pagan creature of sensation and shadow.

Unable to contain it, she gave a soft, sultry laugh full of invitation. "Then *have* me, Dylan," she whispered, knowing she wanted the taste of his real name in her mouth as she made love with him.

Groaning, he lowered his head to her body, licking a path from the tip of her breast, down her midriff, to her belly. After circling her navel with his tongue, he moved lower until his lips were scraping the edge of her curls.

She couldn't contain a moan, or stop her hips from thrusting up a tiny bit in wanton invitation. "Oh, yes."

When he went even lower, delicately licking at her most throbbing, sensitive spot, she almost flew out of her mind. He tasted, gently nibbled, then carefully sucked her until she became nearly incoherent, begging him not to stop and to give her even more.

"Open for me, baby," he growled, dipping lower to lick even more thoroughly.

Then she really did go out of her mind, exploding with pleasure as he devoured her. He was relentless, taking her even higher, not letting her descend from the heights of her orgasm. Spence continued toying with her, tasting her, sliding his fingers over her swollen flesh and taunting her with the promise of what was to come.

"Please," she begged, desperate for more. For deeper contact. "I want to feel you inside me."

Cat shimmied off the bar, her hands on his shoulders, trusting him to hold her. And he did, letting her slide down his body in one long, intimate caress. Facing each other, they both panted and stared for a long, heady moment, knowing the best was yet to come.

Another unexpected moment of silence descended. Then a whir, a click and another song. Faster. With a stronger bass note and a louder drumbeat.

"You choreographed this perfectly," she said.

He tangled his hands in her hair and drew her close. "Just wait until you see what I can do to some Metallica."

Then he caught her mouth in a mind-blowing kiss, deep,

hungry and carnal. They were gasping when it ended. Gasping and reaching blindly for one another. She grabbed his zipper as he thrust a hand into his pocket. Cat shoved his jeans down one second after he retrieved a condom.

"Boy Scout," she said when she saw it.

"No. But I *do* believe in being prepared."

She held her breath, watching with both curiosity and avarice as he pushed his briefs and jeans all the way off. And when she saw him—*really* saw him, so big and hard and ready—she moaned and started to shake.

Glorious. And all hers. At least for tonight.

Sheathing himself, Spence bent and effortlessly lifted her into his arms. She clung to him, her arms around his shoulders, her legs around his waist. His guttural growl told her he was just as affected by the brush of her wet skin against his erection. Pressing openmouthed kisses against his jaw, Cat began to whisper hungry, pleading things in his ear.

"Anything worth having is worth waiting for, Cat," he said, his voice thick and tight as he rubbed against her, teasing her with the promise of his entry but not giving her what she craved.

Whimpering, she tightened her legs around his lean hips and tilted farther, trying to take what he wasn't giving. He laughed softly, kissing her again.

"*Please*, Dylan," she cried against his lips.

"Ah, Cat, I love the way you say my name," he said on a long sigh. Then, cupping the curves of her bottom in his hands, he moved her, lowered her and finally thrust up into her.

Cat dropped her head back and savored the deepness, the tightness, the joining. Sex had never been like this— never. She'd never felt as filled or as cherished or as ravenous as she did with Spence. And her moans probably told him so.

As he began to move, slowly easing out of her body only to drive back in, Cat leaned back against the edge of the bar. Still holding her by the hips, he dropped forward and covered her nipple with his mouth, sucking deeply, and an explosion of warmth and delight surged through her body.

"Cat?" He drew her up again, pulling her tightly against him as he continued his sensual strokes deep inside her.

"Mmm?" was all she could manage.

Pressing a sweet kiss of pure emotion to her lips, he whispered, "This was worth the wait."

OVER THE NEXT FEW DAYS, Dylan did everything he could to help Cat, liking that she really *did* need his help. Despite being certain she'd wanted him to stay for more sensual reasons, she'd also been honest about the amount of work she was facing. There was a lot to do, and frankly, he didn't know how she would have managed it on her own. But he had no doubt she'd have tried.

Thankfully, being a freelance software designer, he didn't have to make a lot of arrangements to walk away from his private life for a while. He had no boss to report to, no family nearby who'd question his absence. No projects that couldn't wait.

And Banks was taking care of his house. The shithead.

His friend had come by Monday at lunchtime, bringing Dylan some clothes and stuff. Meeting him in the parking lot, he'd been about to thank him for doing it. At least, until he saw what his clothes were packed in: the rattiest duffel bag Dylan had ever seen. "If my clothes are infested with crawling creatures, I am going to make you eat them one by one," he'd bitten out.

Banks had laughed, unflappable as always. "It's clean. I actually got it from Jeremy and Josh's basement and I ran it through your washer this morning. Come on, admit it. It definitely suits the wild, reckless rock and roller." Pointing toward Jeremy's Harley, still parked in the corner of the lot, he'd added, "As does that." Then he handed Dylan the keys.

Dylan had rolled his eyes. "What's it gonna cost you for getting Jeremy to leave his baby here?"

Banks's grin had been evil. "It's not costing *me* anything. But you owe the kid one weekend in your house for a party."

He'd nearly groaned. A bunch of teenagers tearing up his house…all so he could claim to own the death-on-wheels vehicle sitting outside Cat's business, which he wouldn't ride in a million years? This was getting ridiculous.

Then he'd thought about the previous night and acknowledged the truth. It was *so* worth it.

Before he'd been able to say anything more, Banks had reached over to the passenger seat of his car. "Here," he'd said, tugging something heavy across his lap while Dylan shouldered the scruffy bag. "I brought you this, too.

When he saw his old banged-up guitar case, Dylan had raised a questioning brow.

"You can't exactly serenade her with your Fender. Need a little more than a bass line for some of the sappy songs you wrote about her back when you were young and hairless."

Dylan could only shake his head. "Serenade?"

Banks nodded, then said, in all seriousness, "I know you're mad as hell at me, but you deserved your shot. Now you have it." He handed the guitar case out the window, adding, "Make something happen, my friend, because there's no doubt in my mind you're gonna love her until the day you die."

Shocked by his normally wise-cracking buddy's serious words, Dylan had taken the guitar and watched as Banks roared out of the parking lot. He'd stood there for a long time, thinking about Banks's crazy claim.

Yeah, he'd loved Cat as a kid and he craved her now. But loving her for the rest of his life? Was is really possible?

And, if so, what was he going to do about it…particularly when Cat learned the truth about who he really was?

He hadn't had much time to dwell on it because Cat had been true to her word and put him right to work. When he wasn't scouring the attic and storage room for treasures or junk—or some things Cat insisted were both—he was packing boxes or hauling trash. Negotiating with a greedy used-furniture broker, he'd made sure the guy agreed to buy what he wanted piece by piece, instead of paying one set price for everything, as he'd originally demanded. That would mean a lot more money for Cat when the sale went through at the end of the month.

She'd been very appreciative. And Lordy, did the woman know how to show it. In more positions than he'd imagined possible.

Inspired by her, er, gratitude, Dylan had begun to research antique lamps on the Internet. That, too, had paid off. He'd found a unique lighting company which specialized in old-fashioned colored glass, and had contacted them about the fixtures over the bar. He'd even found an electrician who specialized in delicate work to remove them once Temptation closed its doors for good. The money from those fixtures alone would keep Cat in the black for a while after she closed down.

She appreciated that, too. Appreciated it so much he really wasn't sure he was gonna be able to walk away on Thursday morning.

Which was saying a lot, considering every other night had been just as miraculous.

Making love with Cat was so perfect, such a part of him now, that it felt more natural to be touching her than not. Wherever they were—in her bed, in the bar, in her living room, in the downstairs kitchen—didn't matter. He hungered for her and she was equally as ravenous.

He'd taken special delight in making another of her fantasies come true Tuesday night. Bringing down some blankets from her apartment, he'd led Cat to the stage and loved her there, with the small spotlights splaying pools of color and light all over their bodies.

It had been incredibly erotic. Made more so by his certainty that what was happening between the two of them was so much more than he could ever have anticipated.

They *both* felt the intense connection, he didn't doubt that. He'd become adept at reading her moods, and she knew exactly what he was feeling. Spending practically every waking—and definitely every sleeping—minute together, they'd gotten to know each other like longtime lovers.

They laughed a lot. They loved a lot. They talked a lot. About everything except the past. Not to mention the future. But he sure had been thinking about them both, wondering how long he could let this go on before he came clean with her.

And what would happen when he did.

7

LATE THURSDAY AFTERNOON, Dylan returned to Temptation after making a trip to a moving supply company. He'd gone to pick up some boxes for Cat to use for packing up her apartment. He found her behind the bar, a smile on her face, hanging up the phone. No one else was around.

"Hey," she said, watching him walk in. Scrunching her brow, she looked doubtfully at the big pile of flattened boxes he dropped onto the table closest to the door. "You do realize I only own a small dresser full of clothes and a mismatched, incomplete set of dishes, don't you?"

Walking over, he raised a challenging brow. "These are for your shoes."

She nibbled her bottom lip. "You peeked into my closet, huh?"

"I've seen less footwear at Payless."

She tossed her head, sending those blond tresses bouncing. "Everyone deserves one decadent indulgence."

You're mine flashed through his head, but he didn't say it.

"Well," he replied instead as he leaned across the bar and ran his fingers through a long, silky lock of her hair. "I'll approve of your vice if you wear those knee-high black patent leather boots for me some night."

"Oooh, you saw those, hmm?" She licked her lips. "They were part of a Halloween costume…but I kept them. Just in case."

"Just in case you wanted to drive a man insane with lust?"

"Well, yeah."

Without being asked, she reached down into the fridge and got him a cold bottle of beer, pushing it toward him. Dylan took it gratefully. He didn't drink much, but when he wasn't performing, he liked an icy beer at the end of the day. She already remembered his brand.

"I must say my shoe wardrobe does seem to come in handy for seduction," she said.

"Oh?" He tensed at the thought of Cat seducing any-one else.

Nodding, she explained, "My friend Gracie who owns the book store next door borrowed a pair of my sexiest shoes last Saturday night."

Gracie's seduction. Not Cat's. Thank heaven.

Dylan had heard about Gracie, as much as he'd heard about Cat's friend Tess and her sister Laine, but he hadn't met any of them yet. Unless… "Gracie—she's not the one with the prosthetic leg, is she?" he asked, thinking about the flamboyantly attractive young woman he'd seen com-ing out of the bookstore yesterday.

Cat shook her head. "That's Trina, her assistant, who is a riot. She was in here a while ago having a big blowout with this guy who spends his days writing in Gracie's store. Then they made up. Big-time. I thought I was gonna have to turn the hose on them." Grinning at the memory, she added, "If you'd met Gracie, you'd remember her—she's got the prettiest eyes you've ever seen."

Dylan doubted that. Seemed to him he was looking at the prettiest eyes he'd ever seen.

"Anyway, she wore the shoes to her ten-year Kendall High reunion the other night."

"Ten years, huh?" Good thing Gracie wasn't one year younger. That would have put her in *his* graduating class—and her memory might be a little better than Cat's.

"Yep. And the shoes apparently brought out the very naughty Gracie who almost never comes out to play."

He winced as she wagged her eyebrows suggestively. "Don't tell me she had one of those reunion hookups. I thought they only happened in chick flicks. Or horror movies."

"And in romance novels," she replied airily. "But yeah, she really did. She came in for lunch on Monday and told me all about her wicked evening in my wickedly hot shoes. It was very exciting, right down to a case of mistaken identity." Emitting a tiny wolf whistle, she added, "And when I met the guy earlier today, I totally got it. He came in looking for her and had a beer. Whoa, mama."

Dylan narrowed his eyes, though he knew she was teasing him. "Oh?"

"Hunk-a-licious." Then, taking mercy on him, she admitted, "Only, he's no rock and roller. Has this upper-crust Boston voice. And he probably likes elevator music or something."

"Horrors," he replied dryly. Then, still amused by her cute effort to make him jealous, he added, "Because I know how you like to move to more *sultry* music."

Her expression grew a little dreamy. "Oh, yes. I like moving and dancing and *living* in rhythm with the sultry stuff."

Perfect. Because so did Dylan.

Thinking about what she'd said about her conversation with her friend, he fished around for some more information. "So, uh, you and Gracie were sharing some big secrets, huh?"

Her eyes twinkled and she didn't answer the question she knew damn well he was asking: whether she'd been talking about *him*. "We always share secrets," she replied with a prim nod.

Twining his fingers into her hair and cupping her head, he tugged her forward and leaned over the bar, meeting her halfway. As their lips came close enough to share a breath, he whispered, "So did you tell her I made you come while you were mixing a couple of mai tais right here behind the bar Monday night?"

She shuddered a little, her lips parting in a tiny gasp of memory. "God, you were so bad to do that to me. I can't imagine what the couple at table four thought about how long it took you to hook up the cable you were *supposedly* working on back here. Or how long it took me to make their drinks."

"I don't imagine they realized I was kissing your bare thighs under your skirt, or that I had my hand on your—"

"Shh," she said, putting her fingers over his lips with a helpless giggle. "Now I know why you told me you wanted to see me in a skirt instead of jeans some night. And that cable story…sheesh, I'm so gullible."

Giving her a wolfish look, he said, "Yeah. You are. As for the couple drinking the mai tais? Well, any guy pansy enough to actually order one in public probably had no *idea* what I was doing to you under there."

"Pansy, huh? Guess that means you won't be ordering a Slippery Nipple anytime soon?"

"No, but I sure as hell plan to serve one."

Unable to resist any longer, he pressed his lips to hers, falling into the same sweet, hot, delightful place he always went when he kissed Cat Sheehan. She tasted like cherries and laughter and sex and sunshine, all rolled into one.

When they pulled apart, she admitted, "By the way, I don't share all my secrets." Half lowering her lashes over her eyes, she added, "Especially not the ones I want to happen again."

He leaned even closer, practically lying on his stomach so he could see all of her. "You wearing a skirt today?"

She stepped back so he could see her sexy, tight jean miniskirt that revealed those endlessly long legs. "And nothing else," she said, pure wickedness in her voice.

At that, Dylan went right over the bar, crawling toward her with deliberation.

"What are you…"

"You awaken the beast, you deal with the consequences," he growled.

She began to giggle as he hopped down beside her. Reaching toward his jeans, she squeezed him lightly, gasping as she realized he was already hard for her. "Well," she said regretfully, "the beast is gonna have to stay in his cage for a while unless he wants to get caught rampaging by any customers who might wander in."

Shaking his head and laughing, he swooped down to kiss her, quick and hard. "I'*m* the beast," he said once he pulled away.

"No, you're the rebel."

Rebel? "Uh, not exactly."

She reached up and rubbed the tip of her index finger across his bottom lip, until he nibbled at it. "You are. From the top of your head to the tip of your boots and every delicious inch in between." Shuddering a little, she leaned against him and cupped his cheek in her hand, tangling her fingers in his hair. "And you drive me crazy. From your eyes to your voice, to the tight way you wear your impossibly soft and threadbare jeans, to the sexy hoop in your ear, you make me absolutely wild."

He wondered if now was a good time to tell her the earring was the magnet kind and his ear wasn't pierced.

Probably not.

Especially because her words bothered him. The intensity in her voice, the hunger in her eyes...they were for Spence. She was no longer talking to Dylan, the man she'd gotten to know all week. She was talking to the homeless rocker she'd taken in Sunday night.

It was ridiculous to be jealous of himself, yet that's exactly what he was feeling.

Before he could do anything about it—and he honestly didn't know what that might have been—the front door swung open. Two women entered, looking around the empty room. Waving them toward one of the dozen vacant tables, Cat stepped back, creating a more sedate distance between them. Her cheeks pinkened and Dylan almost laughed, the blush so unexpected on the face of a woman so sensual and provocative.

"I should go make sure Zeke's still here to cook anything," she murmured. "I've been having him leave around two all week, then come back in at five."

Looked around the empty tavern, he frowned. "Not much of a crowd at all since Sunday night, huh?"

She shook her head. "There were a few people in around noon, like there have been every day this week. The business people still drift in Monday through Friday for lunch since they're downtown, anyway, and don't have to deal with the detour hassles. Nobody else bothers."

A sad, faraway look darkened her expression as the reality of her situation returned full force to her mind. For a little while, he'd succeeded in lightening her mood, making her laugh, making her forget. But the truth of why he was really working here and the uncertainty of her future had returned.

Dylan knew enough about Cat to understand why the closing of Temptation would hurt her. He just hoped his presence in her life was making it easier. And would, perhaps, give her something to look forward to once this was all over. "You okay?"

Inhaling and then releasing a deep breath, she nodded and offered him a tentative smile. "Yeah, I am. Not fabulous, but okay, which is exactly what I was telling my sister right before you walked in."

"Laine?"

Cat nodded. "She called from California. It seems the wildfire threatening my aunt's house is out. Laine offered to come back here."

Laine coming back…that could be a good thing for Cat. But it sure would eliminate her need for *him*. He didn't move a muscle as he waited for her to continue.

"I told her not to," Cat murmured.

His heart started beating again. "Oh?"

"Yeah." She glanced around the room, her expression tender as she studied all the empty tables and the single occupied one. The stage, the jukebox. The windows and the overhead lights. "Don't get me wrong," she finally said, "this totally sucks. But I'm getting used to the idea. I'm…dealing. Even seeing beyond this month and making some plans."

God, he prayed those plans would somehow include him.

"That's thanks to you, Dylan," she said, placing her hand flat on his chest. She stared up at him, emotion shining clearly in her green eyes. "You've given me strength to face all of this without feeling so…abandoned. Once I had your strength behind me, I began realizing I will survive this."

He covered her hand with his own, wondering if she could feel the way his heart was pounding in his chest. Because there had been feeling in her words. And the way she was looking at him now…well, he could live on it for weeks.

"I'm glad you asked me to stay," he admitted.

One of the women at the table cleared her throat, and Cat pulled her hand away. "I'll be right over," she called.

"Guess I'd better get back to work," he said. But before he left to carry the boxes upstairs, he asked, "So, did you happen to tell Laine about having a little help?"

She shook her head. "I want to keep it…close. Private."

"Intimate," he murmured.

"Exactly."

He understood that. Because he was feeling the same way—wanting the rest of the world to just leave them alone for a while. At least long enough for them to figure out where they were going and how they were going to get there.

"All I told Laine was that I'm okay, and that I don't need her back here until the twenty-seventh."

Tilting his head in confusion, Dylan said, "But your last day in business is Sunday the twenty-sixth."

"Yes, it's our last *official* day. But if Temptation's going out, she's going out with a bang, not a whimper. That Monday is going to be an all-day party for everyone who ever cared about this place. Family. Friends. Regulars." Winking, she added, "Musicians."

"I'll be here," he replied tenderly.

"I know you will." Her voice was just as soft. "In fact, I wouldn't want to have it without you."

DESPITE GOING THROUGH one of the most difficult periods of her life, Cat was feeling better than she had in a long,

long time. It was so strange. She was still depressed about
losing Temptation, yet, if asked, she'd have had to answer
that she'd never been happier in her personal life. Because
of Spence.

It's a fling. She kept having to remind herself of that,
though, honestly, she didn't know if what was happening
between them had any sort of name.

Enchantment?

Maybe.

All she knew was that he constantly made her laugh
and made her hot and made her feel protected and definitely not alone.

She'd quickly become accustomed to sleeping beside
him in her bed, sometimes waking up deep in the night,
just looking at him lying there. Perfect and handsome and
amazing, even when asleep.

Sometimes during the day, she'd catch him humming
under his breath and more than once she'd considered
asking him to sing for her. Only for her. But she hadn't…it
seemed almost *too* personal. Too intimate.

And she didn't want to hear him sing her a song that
he'd written for another woman.

Though she kept telling herself she didn't have much
more time—that as soon as Temptation was gone, Spence
likely would be, too—she couldn't help wondering if there
were any chance for them beyond this month. Beyond forever sounded good, too.

Cat forced the hopeful image out of her brain and
looked up as the door opened early Friday afternoon. To
her surprise, Dinah entered the bar. The waitress was
early—she'd been coming in at five all week, though, honestly, tonight was probably the only night Cat would need
the help. Since they had a live country-and-western band

coming in to perform, she expected a crowd of people to actually show up ready to drink and party, unlike every other night this week when a handful of people had shown up ready to die or take a nap.

"Hey, what's up?" she asked the older woman. "Zeke's already gone if you're, you know, on the prowl."

Dinah rolled her eyes. "I've given up on Zeke. The man's blind as a bat if he can't see what a good thing he's got right in front of him."

"He's shy."

Startled by the male voice, Cat whirled around and saw Spence approaching from the back hallway. He'd been working all morning, taking down some old photos and posters, and trying to figure out if there were any way to salvage the beautiful mural Cat had had painted on the wall last year. The same artist who'd done the Temptation signs had created an elaborate piece of artwork that literally embodied the spirit of Temptation.

The Garden of Eden. Complete with fig leaves.

Dinah snorted. "Shy? Ha."

"I mean it," Spence said, sliding up onto one of the stools and reaching for the bottle of water Cat had already pulled out for him. "He asked me yesterday when exactly it became okay for a man to let a woman ask him out on a date."

Color rose in Dinah's cheeks. "I most certainly have not asked him on a date."

"Lemme guess," Cat said, tapping her cheek with the tip of her finger, "you asked him to have sex?" Dinah swatted at her with her handbag and Cat stepped easily out of the way, laughing at the woman's outraged expression. "I'm kidding. I know you're not completely desperate."

Spence sipped from his water bottle. "I think what Zeke was asking was whether it would be okay for him to say yes." Dinah still didn't say anything, so he added, "Just in case someone…anyone…ever *did* ask him out on a date."

The woman's jaw dropped and she patted her hair, looking pleased. "Meaning me?"

"I think so," he said.

Dinah grabbed Spence's face and smacked a loud kiss on his lips. Cat almost laughed as his face reddened the tiniest bit. For someone so sexy and self-assured, the man was sometimes easily disconcerted.

"That was worth coming in here early," Dinah said as she came around behind the bar and tucked her purse away on the bottom shelf.

"Why *did* you come in early?" Cat asked.

"You tell me," Dinah said with a sly look. "I got orders to cover this afternoon."

"Orders?" Frowning in confusion, she glanced at Spence and saw his self-satisfied expression. "Did you…"

"Yeah," he said, not even letting her finish. "I *asked*. Thanks for coming in, Dinah. She deserved an afternoon off."

"An afternoon off?"

"You have parrot tendencies you haven't told me about yet?" he teased.

"The only bird around here is the peacock who works in the kitchen," Dinah said. "And I'm exactly the woman to ruffle his feathers a little bit."

"No doubt about it, beautiful," Spence said.

Dinah preened, then put both of her hands on Cat's back and pushed her out from behind the bar. Ignoring her sputters and protests, Spence reached for her hand and tugged her toward the front door.

"Wait a minute, I can't just leave!"

"Sure you can. Dinah's got it covered."

Outnumbered and outfoxed, Cat had no choice but to allow Spence to tug her toward the front door and out into the bright afternoon sunshine.

"You don't melt or anything in the daylight, do you?" he asked, watching as she squinted.

"I'm a night owl," she admitted. "And a barfly. But this is actually kind of nice."

"So are toaster ovens," he said, shaking his head in bemusement. "Only they're less hot."

Leading her toward the small parking lot behind Temptation, he headed for Cat's little sedan. She dug her feet into the ground. "How about we take your motorcycle instead?"

He followed her pointed stare, already shaking his head. "No way."

"Oh, come on, I'm not scared."

"You should be," he muttered. Shrugging, he added, "And I don't have an extra helmet."

"So we'll live dangerously."

Her words sparked a strong reaction in him because Spence grabbed her upper arms. "No. I don't even want to think about you getting on one of those things *with* a helmet and I'd spank you if you ever did without one."

Fisting her hand, she put it on her hip and cocked a brow. "Well, darlin', if you're trying to talk me out of it, you're doing a piss-poor job."

He stared, got her meaning, and started to sputter. "Cat…"

"I'm kidding." Under her breath, she added, "Pretty much."

Shaking off his arm, she stepped closer to the Harley, sparkling and bright in the sunshine. "It really is a beauty," she said, running her hand over the padded seat. "Sleek and dangerous."

To her surprise, his frown deepened. Weren't guys usually as proud of their rides as they were of what was in their pants?

"Come on," he said. "Do you wanna drive since we're taking your car?"

Giving him a little pout, she tried one more time. "You're sure we can't take this?"

"It's…it's broken-down, remember?"

Oh, yikes. He was red-faced and she almost bit her tongue, remembering what Banks had said the other night. The bike wasn't running well and Spence obviously didn't have the money to get it repaired.

She was such an idiot. A whiny idiot, playing girlie games when the man obviously had too much pride to admit what the real problem was. Without another word, she slid her arm in his and led him to her car, getting in on the passenger side.

He got in and started the engine, his jaw still tight.

"Look, Spence, I'm sorry," she said, needing him to know she understood. "I totally forgot it was broken-down. After I pay you for working here, you'll have the money to…"

His head swung around, his eyes blazing as he snapped, "You're not paying me a cent."

"But, you're working for me…"

"I'm sleeping with you," he bit out.

"Yes, at night. But during the day…"

"Cat, I am *not* taking your money."

Now it was her turn to stiffen. She wasn't a charity case. "We had a deal. You know I wouldn't have let you do so much if I hadn't planned to pay you for it."

He didn't relent or soften a bit. "That was before you took me into your bed. When I was going to sleep on the cot, it was a job. Now I'm sleeping in your arms. I'm not some damn gigolo who's gonna take money for helping out the woman he's involved with."

She shivered a bit, never having seen the man so utterly furious. He was something to see when he was angry—so big and loud and strong. Yet she wasn't frightened, because she knew he'd never hurt her. She just couldn't help feeling a little intimidated. But she also understood his point of view.

Spence was every bit as proud as she was. And while she wouldn't accept his charity, he wouldn't take her money. Stalemate.

Unless…unless she found another way to compensate him, without him even being aware of it until it was done. Already feeling better, she began wondering which of her customers were mechanics at some of the local garages. Determined to make some calls in the next few days and find someone who could fix Spence's motorcycle, she gave him one small nod of agreement.

"Okay," she said softly, letting him think he'd won this round. "I won't try to pay you again."

"Good."

"But you need to eat more."

Giving her a curious look, he put the car in gear and pulled out of the parking space. "Why?"

"Well," she said, "if all you're getting is room and board, it's not really fair for me to feed you nothing but Zeke's cheeseburgers."

He didn't say anything for a long moment, and she saw his hands tighten reflexively on the steering wheel. Then, in a low, intense voice, he said, "You've definitely been feeding me more than that."

At first, her mind went straight to the naughty possibilities of his comment. But the way he'd said it made her suspect he hadn't been referring to the way he'd been devouring her every night this week in her bed.

And for the rest of the car ride, she couldn't help wondering what he'd meant.

DYLAN HAD NEVER BEEN more angry at himself for allowing this charade to happen than he was when they pulled out of Temptation's parking lot. The motorcycle story was so ridiculous. But so was everything else, wasn't it?

He had a BMW parked in a garage a few blocks away, owned a two-story house in the next town, had a healthy portfolio, a healthier bank account…and was playing the part of a homeless bum. *The things we do for love.*

That word—love—bounced around in his brain as he and Cat drove through the streets of Kendall.

Yeah. He loved her. He couldn't even try to fool himself that this was some dumb crush left over from high school, or that it was just about sex. If he'd never laid eyes on her before last Friday night, he'd still have fallen just as hard.

Cat Sheehan fed his soul—which was exactly what he'd been thinking when she'd laughingly told him to eat more. And he wasn't sure he'd ever feel complete again if she were to walk out of his life.

Which put him in one hell of a position. He didn't want to keep up this ridiculous charade, but he couldn't honestly predict how she'd act when she found out the truth. For all he knew, she'd kick him out the door. Which would be bad enough in terms of his love life. It would be even worse for Cat in terms of her workload.

He'd gotten a lot accomplished this week…but not enough. Not nearly enough. Cat needed him and, frankly, he needed her. And he wasn't willing to risk that by confessing his sins. Not yet. Soon…but not yet.

"So where are we going, anyway?" she asked, breaking the silence in the car.

"It's a surprise."

"Is it the type of surprise that's going to get me back to Temptation by five for the happy hour crowd we might actually get tonight?"

He nodded. "You'll be back in time."

They didn't talk much during the rest of the drive, except when he pulled onto the highway and Cat guessed they were headed for Austin. They were, but she hadn't guessed where.

She began fishing. "We going to the tattoo parlor where I got mine so you can get a matching one?"

Snorting, he shook his head. "Uh, sorry, no needles entering this body unless they contain vaccines against various diseases or pain-numbing agents when I'm at the dentist."

Cocking a brow, she stared at his earlobe. "Ahem."

Without saying a word, Dylan reached up, stuck his finger into the silver loop and tugged. The two-part, magnetic earring gave way, falling to the console between the seats.

"You…you cheater!" she sputtered.

Laughing at the indignation on her face, he said, "You think I'm crazy enough to intentionally have someone poke unnecessary holes in my body? Josh and Jeremy's little sister decided that the long-haired rebel of the group really needed an earring so she gave me this one."

"You're a big phony," she said, beginning to laugh. "This is serious ammunition, you know. Next time some horny bar tramp throws her shirt at you, I might just tell her you're a big fraud with a fake earring."

Fraud. Yeah. That was him. His body tensed, his good humor dissipating. It was easy to forget he was just play-acting for a little while, but the truth always came back with a roar. He was a phony in just about every way, and God only knew what Cat was going to say about it when she found out.

Maybe she'll laugh, like she did about the earring.

Yeah. And maybe it was gonna snow right here in Kendall, Texas, next Christmas.

"Well," Cat said, apparently not noticing his distraction, "I think it's very sexy, pierced or not." She dug around between the seats and came up with both parts of the earring. Without asking, she leaned over and put the thing back on, tenderly brushing the tips of her fingers over his neck, blowing warm breaths on his skin.

When she kissed him there, tracing her tongue over his pulse point, he nearly growled. "I'm gonna drive off the road unless you go back to your side of the car."

She nearly purred. "Oooh, yeah, car sex at a rest stop." Dropping her hand on his leg, she slid it up, getting dangerously close to his suddenly very alert crotch.

"Cat," he said with a groan, "I meant I'm going to *crash*."

Not relenting, she continued to kiss and nibble his neck, her hand moving ever higher until her fingertips were an inch away from very serious trouble and a potential wreck.

He dropped his hand over hers, muttering, "Enough. We have someplace to go."

"So tell me where we're going and I'll stop."

Quickly glancing over, he saw the mischief in Cat's expression and knew she was still very curious about where they were headed. "You'll see when we get there."

"When's that?"

"You're relentless, aren't you?"

Removing her hand to safer territory, she nodded, waiting for him to explain. But he didn't give her even a tiny hint, not until he pulled up to the entrance of the university a short time later.

"Here?" she asked, her eyes nearly popping out of her head. "We're going to the University of Texas?"

That's exactly where they were going. Cat had talked about going back to school, and he'd noticed the application packet she'd received in the mail Monday. But she'd hidden it away, as if embarrassed, and hadn't even begun to work on it. He suspected he knew why—she needed a push, some encouragement, a reason to fill the thing out. A reason to believe she wasn't just grasping at some pipe dream and that she really could do something completely unexpected with her life.

Dylan parked the car in a lot outside the administration building. Thankfully, since it was summer session, the campus was much less crowded, because he'd heard parking was a nightmare during the rest of the year. "So," he said as he cut the engine, "you think we can pass for a couple of eighteen-year-olds?"

She eyed him up and down, appearing skeptical. "I doubt it. If I ever did register here, I'd stick out like a sore thumb, even if I really was eighteen."

Reaching over, he took her hand in his and squeezed it. "You'd stick out like a gorgeous blonde and every young college dude would be all over you. Don't think that hasn't occurred to me, so you really ought to be rewarding me for my mature lack of jealousy." Giving her a lascivious look, he added, "Sexual favors are always an appropriate reward."

She wasn't teased out of her sudden bad mood. "It's not just my age that'll make me stick out."

"What do you mean?"

Cat kept looking out the window, staring at the buildings, the grounds, the people milling around—obviously students taking summer classes. Her sigh was probably audible to those standing by the tower, which was a landmark on campus. "I belong in a bar slinging drinks and fending off pervs. Not on a college campus." Shaking her head, she lowered her voice. "And certainly not sitting behind a teacher's desk in a high-school classroom."

This doubting woman was *so* not the Cat the rest of the world knew. That woman had boatloads of confidence—with good reason, given her looks, her personality and her wit.

Right now, he suspected, he was sitting with the Cat few people ever saw. The wistful one. The quiet one. The one who doubted her own abilities, her own intelligence. The one who sometimes seemed so alone.

The one he'd first begun to understand by the light of a bonfire so many years ago.

He lifted his hand to her face, running the tips of his fingers across her cheek, then gently taking her chin to make her look at him. She met his stare, her expression serious and her eyes clear. He certainly hadn't expected tears—Cat was not the sort to feel sorry for herself. Neither, however, had expected this absence of emotion.

"Cat, you have so much potential, and you have every right to do whatever you can to make your dreams come true." She opened her mouth to speak, but he touched his index finger to her lips. "I'm not trying to push you into anything, and if you want me to start the car and drive away, I will. But I wish you'd get out and walk around with me, just for a little while, to see how it feels. Then maybe you'll be more interested in filling out the application that came in the mail the other day."

"You noticed that, huh?"

"I noticed. And since you requested it, I have to assume

you wanted it. So why not look around and get yourself pumped up about it, instead of hiding it in your underwear drawer?"

She crossed her arms and lifted a brow. "Why, exactly, were you looking in my underwear drawer?"

He rolled his eyes. "Because your washer's on the fritz and I ran out of shorts."

She snickered, her mood finally lightening. "Well, if you want to borrow my panties, you could at least *ask*."

"Forget it," he said with a mock growl as he leaned across the console to nuzzle the side of her neck. "I'd rather go commando. Gotta leave your panties alone, since your supply is running pretty low."

She tilted her head to the side and moaned from somewhere low in her throat. He followed the sound, kissing his way along her skin.

"If I am," she murmured, "it's only because *someone* keeps ripping them off me."

He chuckled. "That's only because *someone* is so sexy I can't stop myself."

Nibbling his way up her delicate neck, he finally pressed his lips to hers in a warm, wet kiss meant to both arouse her and give her confidence. They only pulled apart when they heard shouts and whooping from outside. Some of the students had apparently noticed.

"Well, now you really fit in on a college campus," he said.

He almost held his breath, waiting for her response. If she asked him to drive away, he'd do so, though not without feeling the slightest bit disappointed in her.

Finally, she nodded. "Okay. Let's go check out the campus."

8

THE COUNTRY-AND-WESTERN GROUP Cat had hired for the weekend wasn't as popular as Dylan's band had been, but they weren't bad. Not bad at all. They'd certainly had her feet tapping for three nights in a row as she worked the bar, making the drinks as fast as Dinah could place the orders.

She figured the fact that the musicians were middle-aged and paunchy had something to do with the shortage of young, on-the-make women in the audience. Still, they put on a good show, and they entertained the small crowd that did come in each night. She'd sold lots of drinks and earned a lot of tips and made Kendall's line dancers really happy.

To give him credit, Spence hadn't shown any distaste for the whole thing. She'd figured, given his passion for rock and roll, that he wasn't into country. Actually, he didn't mind it. It was the line dancing he hated, which she discovered Sunday night when she tried to nudge him out into the dancing crowd he'd successfully managed to avoid on the previous two nights.

"Go on, give the single women out there a thrill," she said when he moseyed behind the bar to offer her a hand.

As if she'd let him make his famous margarita for any other female. And definitely not a Slippery Nipple…which she was still counting on him to deliver one of these nights.

"You must be joking."

"You don't like country-and-western music?"

"I like almost any music, except opera. Country-and-western's fine," he said. "Line dancing, however, is for saps and old ladies at wedding receptions."

Grinning, she gestured toward the younger women in the room who were shaking it with gusto. "They're not all old. And they've been eyeing you up all night, sitting there in the corner nursing one beer. Go on, give them a thrill."

His frown deepened. "I'd rather put on a thong and do the mambo than line dance to 'Achy Breaky Heart.'"

"Well, I don't want you giving them *that* much of a thrill."

A grin tickled his lips.

Turning to face a customer waiting to place his order on the other side of the bar, she gave him a wicked look over her shoulder. "What is it with you and women's underwear, anyway?"

She should have known better than to taunt him. Because Spence stepped right up behind her, tucking in close so that the warmest, hardest parts of his front was pressed right against her back and bottom. She hissed, feeling heat rush into her cheeks. But he didn't relent. Instead, he reached around and snaked one arm across her waist, then nuzzled the side of her neck. "How many times do I have to tell you," he said with a hungry growl, "I haven't ripped them off you every single night this week because I want to *wear* them."

Judging by his roar of laughter, the customer—a long-time regular who'd stuck with them through the construction—had overheard. He tilted back his cowboy hat and smacked his hand flat on the surface of the bar. "Oooh, Cat Sheehan, I never thought I'd see the day."

"What day is that, Earl? The day somebody mistook that rug under your hat for real hair?"

He snorted, impossible to offend. "Nope. The day a man got you so wound up you made my Jack and Coke with gin and Sprite."

Glancing down in horror, Cat realized she had, indeed, mixed that unappetizing concoction. Scrunching her eyes shut, she mumbled, "Sorry about that. Next one's on the house."

Earl shrugged, his good humor never fading from his round face. "Not a problem. It's worth every penny to see you looking at someone else the way most of the fellers usually look at *you*."

Cat nibbled her lip, then tried to stare him into silence. "I don't know what you're talking about. Maybe you've had enough, Earl. You better watch it or I'll have to cut you off."

Uncowed, the older man winked at Spence. "She's got the young men all chompin' at the bit and pantin' for her attention, and she never gives any of 'em the time of day." Then, eyes twinkling, he added, "Nice to see your heart ain't froze up solid, little girl."

Cat winced, wishing the floor would open up so she could sink into it. She'd just been accused of being a heartless tease in front of Spence. Could've been worse, she supposed. Being called a tease in front of your lover was probably better than being called a tramp.

"Cheers, y'all," Earl said as he scooped up his new drink, which Cat had just made, and wandered back toward his table, his shit-kicker boots clomping on the wood floor.

"You better watch it, Earl," she called after the laughing man, "or I'll uninvite you from our closing-down party next Monday."

He turned on his heel and wagged his index finger at her. "You're not keeping me away from that shindig, darlin'. I'll come say goodbye to Sheehan's Pub even if I have to crash the party."

Grinning at the man, who'd been a loyal customer way back when her dad had been working behind the bar, Cat nodded and then got back to work, struggling to get caught up with the multitude of drink orders.

The rest of the evening flew by until it was last call and the band started packing up for the night. Rubbing a weary hand over her brow, Cat watched the customers drift out, savoring their good humor and their friendly waves. They were like family, some of them. Like Earl. Another reason saying goodbye to Temptation in another week was going to be brutal.

"You okay?" Spence asked after everyone else was gone and they were alone in the closed tavern. He'd been helping her put up the chairs and sweep the floor. Well, actually, she'd swept and he'd held the dustpan.

"I'm fine. It was a good night."

"Made a lot?"

She shrugged. "Not a fortune. But the feeling was good. You know?"

Thinking about it, he slowly nodded. "Yeah, I think I know what you mean. There's a real camaraderie, isn't there?"

"Exactly." Her chest suddenly felt tight. "I'm going to miss a lot of those people."

He stepped close, taking the broom from her hand and leaning it in a corner. "They'll miss you, too." Tugging her into his arms, he stroked her hair, then her back, trailing his fingers down her spine to cup her bottom.

Cat's melancholy mood immediately disappeared as a new kind of tension—the Spence kind of tension—took its place.

"Cat, do you remember last week when you told me about some of the things you wanted to do before you left this place for good?"

Nodding lethargically, she said, "Yes. Like dancing on the bar." She couldn't keep a dreamy sigh from her lips. "And lying on the stage under all those different spotlights. Have I told you yet how much I liked that?"

"I think the whole street heard how much you liked that Tuesday night," he said with a wolfish chuckle.

"Ha ha. I think you were doing some moaning yourself."

"No question about it. Now, back to your fantasies...."

"Yes?"

He kissed her temple, then the top of her cheekbone, then the top of her ear. She started to sigh, then to moan when he nibbled his way to her earlobe.

"How about we make another one come true?"

DYLAN HAD TRIED TO THINK of a way to make Cat's nude sunbathing fantasy come true, but it'd been impossible. Somebody was always around—or there was the potential of somebody always being around. Whether it was a bar customer, Dinah, Zeke or one of the employees of the book store, there was a good chance someone could glance out a window and see whatever was going on in the walled garden out back at any time of the day.

And call him greedy, but he didn't want anyone else seeing Cat reclining naked in the backyard, soaking up the sun. Just him.

So he'd modified things a bit. Because despite how many people were on the premises during the daylight hours...only he and Cat were here late at night. He'd specifically planned for this night, Sunday, since the bar closed down at midnight instead of 2 a.m.

He only hoped soaking up moonlight would be a good enough substitute.

"Where are we going?" she asked, excitement in her voice as he took her hand and led her through the deserted downstairs.

"You'll see." He'd set things up earlier in the day, knowing she'd be much too busy to wander outside.

Earlier this week, Cat had told him how much she regretted that her hectic schedule denied her many chances to retreat out back alone, as she liked to do. Once he'd explored the garden, he'd understood why. It was a wild and tangled oasis, something he'd never have expected in this busy downtown area. He'd sat outside a couple of times, watching the hummingbirds zipping in and out, drinking from the fragrant blooms of coral honeysuckle. So yes, he could see how she would like hiding away out there to lose herself in thought.

Tonight, she was going to lose herself. But it wasn't going to be in thought. It would be in sensuality.

Walking through the back hallway, past the beautiful erotic mural painted on the wall, he slid an arm around her waist.

"We going to the ladies' room?"

"Uh-uh."

When they got to the back door, he unlocked it and stepped outside into the hot, humid night. Thankfully, a slight breeze had kicked up this evening so the still, sultry air was circulating a bit. Enough to enable him to catch the scent of the sweet-smelling honeysuckle, flowering in profusion on the wildly curling vines.

He paused on the back step, examining the garden by night. The dense shrubs, unpruned, grew in all shapes along the base of the tall, limestone garden walls. The vines and moss completed the illusion that the pale stone wall was actually green and alive. A few tall live oak trees dripping with moss provided shade, shadow and mystery. In one corner stood a small statue of a frolicking Cupid, and nearby, a birdbath, the chips in the stone and the brackish color of the water well-suited to the atmosphere of the place.

The garden, which Cat had told him had been planted and maintained by her grandmother, was like an abandoned paradise, long forgotten about except by a chosen few. A good place to be alone. Which, he supposed, was why Cat liked it so much.

"Oh, my goodness," she said as she spied the reclining lawn chair he'd brought out earlier. Surrounded on all sides by the lush, overgrown vegetation, the chair was covered with a brightly colored beach towel. On a small table nearby stood a pitcher of lemonade and two glasses, plus a CD player and a bottle of suntan lotion. Faint strains of music laid down a low, pulsing beat in the otherwise quiet night.

He cast a quick glance toward the other pitcher—the one he'd brought out just a little while ago when she was locking up. It remained discreetly tucked on the ground behind the chair, to be retrieved very soon.

"I can't believe you did this," she said as she stepped closer to the chair.

"You can't sunbathe naked. Will moonbathing do?"

Instead of answering him, she reached for the bottom of her shirt, pulling it up and over her head in one smooth, fluid motion. Dylan watched, his mouth suddenly dry. It went drier when she reached around to unfasten her bra, then tossed that to the ground, too.

"Hmm," he said, stroking his chin, "I don't believe the phrase was sunbathing topless. I think there was full nudity involved."

Laughing, Cat kicked off her shoes and unfastened her jeans. He held his breath, watching as she pushed them down. No matter how many times he'd seen her body in the past week, the view always thrilled him. She was perfect—softly curved, creamy-skinned, full-breasted and long-legged. His fantasy woman.

But he suspected she would still be his fantasy woman in thirty years when her body had a few more pounds, a few wrinkles, and maybe, God willing, stretch marks from the babies he wanted to have with her.

Dylan shook the images out of his mind. He knew he was in love with Cat and wanted to marry her, but he couldn't even begin to try to make that happen until he'd come clean with her about everything.

Which he'd do. Soon. But definitely not tonight.

"Are you going to join me?" she asked as she slowly lowered herself onto the recliner and gave him a welcoming look.

"Not yet." Moving closer, he knelt beside her and reached for the bottle of suntan lotion. "Roll over and let me do your back."

Excitement flashed in her eyes, lit so beautifully by the bright moonlight, and she immediately did as he asked. Lying on her stomach, she turned her head to the side to watch him.

He had to pause for minute to appreciate the sculpted lines of her shoulders, the smoothness of her back and the perfect curves of her ass. After brushing her long hair out of the way, he flipped open the top of the bottle with his thumb.

"Don't want you to get burned," he murmured.

"I think I'm going to go up in flames before this night is over."

He laughed softly. "I'm counting on it."

Squeezing some of the lotion into his palm, he hesitated for the briefest second, building her anticipation. Finally, he lowered his hands to her back. She moaned, low and deep, when he began kneading the silky smooth fluid into her skin. Her eyes drifted closed as he made applying sunscreen more of a massage, easing the tension from her shoulders and the back of her neck.

Soon, the lotion disappeared, soaking into her, but it left a fruity, coconut scent in the air. The smell mixed with the heady aroma of the honeysuckle growing all around them, creating a feast for the senses. Just like everything else about this night was going to do.

Bringing the bottle up again, he squeezed it directly onto Cat, letting the milky white fluid drip onto the base of her spine.

"Ooh," she murmured without opening her eyes.

Dylan reached down and brushed his fingertip through the lotion, letting it glide down her hips. Then he massaged it in, taking special delight in hearing her coos as he kneaded her bottom and the backs of her legs.

When he'd finished, right down to the soles of her feet, he said, "Roll over."

"Oh, absolutely."

He hid a smile, knowing how much she liked to be touched, and exactly *where* she liked to be touched. Her breasts were especially sensitive…but he had something other than tanning lotion in store for them.

Not telling her that, he began to massage her again—the front of her shoulders, then down her sides to her midriff. He ignored her breasts completely, hearing her disappointed hiss. Unable to contain an evil chuckle, he applied more sunscreen, gently rubbing her midriff, her soft belly, then that most vulnerable, tender area below her tan line.

She arched up instinctively, but he didn't give her the touch she craved. Instead he continued stroking her, all the way down her legs to the tips of her toes.

"You're a horrible tease," she mumbled throatily.

"No, actually, I'm a very good tease."

"Yeah. But, uh, Mr. Tease, I think you missed a few spots."

He began to kiss a path back up her legs. "Which spots would those be?"

She squirmed a little, her hips rising helplessly as he brushed his mouth up her thigh, over her hip, then onto her belly. She groaned. "Dylan…."

He ignored her, even when she tangled her fingers in his hair. With an impatient sigh, she grabbed for his shirt, tugging it up and off, not even waiting for his help. Then she reached for his waistband.

He tsked. "Ah, ah, I'm not finished lotioning you up yet."

"No kidding. The most vulnerable, sensitive, pale skin on my body didn't get protected. I could get moon poisoning."

Looking up into her eyes, he saw her cock a brow, daring him to deny it. Which he had absolutely no intention of doing.

He raked a hot gaze across her body, focusing mostly on her breasts, topped with her hard, dusky nipples.

Then he reached for the hidden pitcher—the one behind the birdbath. "This calls for some extra special moisture," he murmured as he removed the lid.

Without warning, he drizzled the butterscotch-smelling concoction across her breasts, swirling it deliberately over her distended nipples, positively drenching her in the stuff. "I think I'm going to like this," he said, wondering if she'd realized yet what he'd doused her with.

Without another word, he bent toward her breast and

caught her creamy nipple in his mouth, sucking deeply, letting the flavors of Irish Cream and butterscotch liqueur blend with the delicious taste of Cat.

"Oh, my God," she groaned.

"This is definitely slippery." he said with a chuckle.

"You're wicked."

"You're getting sticky."

He stopped talking for a moment, focusing only on licking and sucking each drop of the creamy drink off every curve of her breast. She began to moan, jerking a little with every strong pull of his mouth, each flick of his tongue.

"I think it made more than your nipples slippery," he said as he tasted his way down her middle. Then, just to make absolutely sure of it, he picked up the pitcher and drizzled a thin line from her belly down into the curls between her legs.

She jerked so hard she almost fell off the chair. "Dylan, you're making me crazy."

"Good." Because she'd been making him crazy for almost a decade. "Whoops. Definitely getting sticky here," he whispered. "I'm going to need to lick every nook and cranny."

"Nook?" she said weakly.

"And cranny."

Lowering his mouth, he followed the gooey line until he reached that sweet spot between her legs. Not even pausing, he licked her thoroughly, drinking up every bit of moisture. Until she came with a cry of delight right against his tongue.

"Oh, yes," she moaned, still shaking and rolling her head back and forth as the pleasure racked her body. "I love the way you do that."

"Then you're gonna adore what I do next." Almost frenzied now to have her—to plunge into her and lose his mind—he grabbed a condom and loosened his jeans, not even taking the time to take them all the way off. Cat opened her eyes to watch, parting her legs invitingly as he sheathed himself.

And Dylan dove right in.

Oh, yes. She was so tight, so wet. Felt so welcoming—like coming back to the place he belonged.

Cat rocked up to meet his thrust, wrapping her legs around his hips and her arms around his neck. "I can't believe you did all this." She kissed his jaw, then his neck. "Thank you."

"You're welcome. So welcome. God, Cat, you feel so good," he said, savoring the sensation of Cat's body wrapped around his own from top to bottom, and *especially* in the middle.

They slowed the pace, rocking into one another, exchanging slow, deep, wet kisses and slower, tender touches. Until finally, with a guttural cry to the full moon overhead, Dylan took them both hurtling over the edge.

CAT FILLED OUT the application to the university Monday and got it in the mail Tuesday. Spence didn't comment, though he knew what she was doing. When he'd heard her groaning as she tried to remember some of the courses she'd taken in high school, he'd given her shoulder a squeeze of encouragement, but hadn't said anything. It was as if he knew she needed to do this completely on her own, but wanted to remind her she had his support.

She hoped she could get in, but if not, there was always community college. Either way, she *was* going to get an education.

That got her thinking about Dylan's future, his dreams

and ambitions. She'd asked him a couple of times if he was happy with his life and where he was going, and each time he'd ducked out of answering. Once by saying he'd never been happier because he'd become involved with her. That had made her heart race. The other time, he'd grown quiet and introspective, murmuring something about her not knowing everything about his past.

Made her wonder if he was a corporate dropout or something. He certainly had the brains and drive to be a successful professional. Plus, he wouldn't be the first person who decided he really wanted to be a rock star instead of a lawyer or accountant and threw it all away to pursue his dreams. She wanted to know more, but Spence had seemed uncomfortable talking about it, so Cat hadn't pushed.

One thing she *did* finally work up the nerve to do was ask him to play for her.

Walking into her bedroom after her shower Wednesday morning, she found him sitting on her bed, strumming his guitar and singing very softly under his breath. He looked amazing, reclining against her pillows, wearing nothing but a pair of jeans. From his wet, fresh-from-his-own-shower hair, over his broad chest still glistening and damp, down to his bare feet, he was the picture of luscious male. And she instantly got hungry and warm, wanting to dive on him and get him all dirty and sweaty again so they'd each have to take another shower. Together.

"There's that song again," she murmured as she leaned against the doorjamb, watching him.

"Sorry," he said, lowering the guitar.

"No! Please, don't stop. I'd...I'd like to hear you. I haven't heard you play anything but your bass."

"I play a little of everything," he said as he brought the guitar back up into position and began to play it again.

The way his fingers moved over the instrument, stroking and flicking and plucking, made her shake a little, remembering the times he'd played her body in exactly that
same way. Sighing, she closed her eyes and listened for a
moment. "Sing that song for me, would you?" she asked,
unable to resist.

There was silence for a moment, and when Cat opened
her eyes, it was to find Spence watching her intently.

"You know which one I mean," she said.

He nodded once. Saying nothing, he began to pick out
the melody, already familiar to her, then started to sing the
lyrics. Somehow, without the backup of the band and the
wild, partying audience, the song seemed more intense.
Much more personal. Much more sensual. And when he
reached the chorus, repeating the line, "the girl with the
fire in her eyes," she nearly melted right there on the spot.

He must have been crazy for that woman. Crazy with
emotion and with want, because both were so clear in
every word, in every note.

Which hurt. She *hated* that he'd written that soul-surren-
dering piece of music for someone else. That he'd loved
someone else that much.

She was jealous. Jealous of someone he said he'd never
really been involved with, someone who was gone from
his life. It wasn't his possible involvement with the woman
that hurt. Cat was no angel, and she sure didn't expect
Spence to have been a monk. Sex with people in the past
she could deal with.

Complete, intoxicating love? Well, that was just a bit
harder to swallow. So much so that when he was done,
she gave him a grateful smile that hid her true thoughts,
then grabbed her clothes and darted back into the bathroom to dress.

"Cat?" he called. "Did I hurt your eardrums or something?"

"No, no, it was great. I just...I just have things to do."

She held her breath, wondering if he'd follow her. After several long moments of silence, she heard him moving around, then heard the door to her apartment opening—and closing.

Staring into the mirror, she stood there for several minutes, wondering why the thought of Spence loving someone else, even before he'd met her, was so painful.

She had some suspicions. But she was nowhere ready to admit them, even to herself.

After drying her hair and pulling on her clothes, she left the apartment to look for him. The man deserved a thankyou...and an explanation. Not an *honest* one, but she had to tell him *something*, so she scoured Temptation. Not having any luck, she finally decided to check out back. That was where she found him.

She'd gotten used to Spence taking care of all the little things that needed to be taken care of around here, but this really surprised her. He was in the garden, squatting by the Cupid statue, going at it with a scrub brush and a bottle of bleach. Beside him was the newly scrubbed birdbath, which looked cleaner than it had in years. "What are you doing with those?"

"Cleaning them up," he replied.

"You really think they're worth salvaging?"

He looked up, meeting her gaze. "Absolutely."

Cat smiled a little, knowing why he was going to this trouble. It had everything to do with the magical hours they'd spent in the garden Sunday night. As if he wanted to hold on to a tangible reminder so the memory of it wouldn't fade.

She didn't think her memories of that night were *ever* going to fade. Among all the incredible moments she'd shared with Spence since she'd met him, their garden interlude would likely remain the strongest in her mind.

One thing was for sure—she'd never be able to drink a Slippery Nipple again, and she wasn't sure she'd ever be able to serve one. Because for the rest of her life, she suspected even the smell of it would probably make her have an orgasm on the spot.

"Spence? Thank you for playing for me. I'm sorry if I acted as though I didn't like it."

He said nothing, just watching her curiously, as if knowing she had more to say.

Taking a deep breath, she admitted the truth. "This is going to sound really stupid."

"Try me."

She stepped closer to the birdbath, running her fingers over the bright, clean edge of the bowl, not meeting his gaze. "Well, I just had this insane moment of jealousy. Silly, huh? But for a second there, I would cheerfully have scratched the fire right out of the eyes of that girl you wrote the song for."

To give him credit, he looked completely stunned. As if he'd expected her to say anything else. "You're...you're serious?"

She nodded, feeling a flush of embarrassment in her cheeks. "I'm sometimes, uh, not very ladylike, and can be, uh...a little ungracious in my thoughts. Particularly when I think of some other woman you wanted as much as you obviously wanted her."

Dropping the scrub brush, he slowly rose to his feet, brushing off the front of his jeans, which were splashed with water and algae. "Cat, you don't understand. That girl...that song..."

Cat put her hand up, stopping him. "Spare me the gory details, please."

Stepping closer, he said, "It was *years* ago."

Knowing he was about her age, she found that difficult to believe. Her skepticism obviously showed.

"Honest to God, I wrote that song when I was fifteen."

Her jaw dropped. Fifteen? He'd had that much talent— not to mention that much mature emotion—and *desire*— at the age of fifteen? "Wow."

"Exactly. And like I told you before, it was definitely a case of unrequited interest. I've never felt that strongly about a *woman* during any of my adult relationships." Something flickered in his eyes and his voice dropped. "Only you."

Somehow, the already sunny morning seemed to get a little sunnier and Cat couldn't contain a big, wide smile. "Whew!"

He laughed, apparently amused by her very visible relief. Taking her hand, he said, "So you ready to take a break? I want to take you out to lunch."

"You won't let me pay you a penny even though you're working like a dog," she said with a scowl, "and you think I'm going to let you take me out to lunch?"

He grinned. "Okay, *you* take *me* out. I'm getting a little sick of Zeke's burgers."

Unable to resist his good humor, she nodded. "Let me make sure Dinah's okay covering the ghost-tavern, and then give me a half hour to get changed."

Though she didn't tell Spence, she also remembered she had some calls to make. Over the last couple of days, between the college paperwork and the incredible lovemaking, Cat had let the issue of Spence's salary slip her mind.

She completely understood his reluctance to take

money from her, considering they were lovers. Since she would have felt exactly the same way, she couldn't blame him. But she wasn't going to let him do all of this for nothing but some mind-blowing sex.

Definitely mind-blowing.

Reminded now of his situation, she was more determined than ever to sneak his keys away, then get someone to work on his bike. When he was finished here, Spence deserved to ride away on a working machine.

Ride away. Lord, she didn't want to think about that, didn't want to even consider it. After next Thursday, when she closed the door to Temptation behind her for the very last time, there would be no more reason for Spence to stay around.

Which had been exactly what she'd wanted, right? Exactly the right thing to happen, given her new commitment to school and settling down to work toward her more responsible future.

So why did it feel so horribly wrong?

"You're an absolute fool, Cat Sheehan," she whispered as she walked back into the bar.

Because she'd gone and done the unthinkable. She'd fallen for him—totally, completely and irrevocably.

How on earth she ever could have imagined it would be safe to have a wild fling with Spence, she didn't know. This was in no way a wild fling. Fling didn't come close to describing the importance of this relationship.

It killed her to even whisper it in her own brain, but she very seriously suspected she was in love for the first time in her life with a guy who would soon be roaring out of it.

9

On Thursday morning, Cat noticed that the shipment she'd ordered from her liquor supplier hadn't shown up. It wasn't too surprising that she hadn't figured it out earlier since she'd been so busy. Aside from the bar, she'd begun packing up her apartment, as well as finding a new one—which hadn't been too big a deal since she'd lived in Kendall all her life. She already had a good idea where she wanted to live and a single visit to a local apartment complex had settled that issue.

But between the packing and the planning and the phone calls, she hadn't even noticed the delivery man hadn't made it on Monday to restock Temptation after the weekend. The guy had been as regular as clockwork for three years, so it hadn't sunk into her brain that she hadn't seen him, not until last night. A decent-size crowd had come in—for the third night in a row—and the shortages had become obvious.

Cat figured the crowd was a result of this weekend's closing. Word had apparently spread, and old customers were drifting in each night to say goodbye. She saw many faces she hadn't seen since the road project began.

But because of those thirsty patrons, she was now totally tapped out of two of her house beers, and was dangerously low on her house brands of liquor.

She was about to reach for the phone to call and raise some hell about it when it rang on its own.

"Temptation," she said.

"I did something wild."

It took her a second to identify the voice as her sister's, because *Laine* and *wild* just didn't normally go together in a sentence. "Uh, wild? You?"

"I got engaged."

Cat's jaw dropped, and so did the receiver. She fumbled around with it for a second, then yanked it back toward her ear. "To who?" she asked, still reeling at the unexpected news.

"That guy I dated years ago, when I lived with Aunt Jen for the summer. His name is Steve. Wanna come to a wedding on Saturday?"

Saturday? Cripes, not only was her sister getting married, she was practically eloping! This was so not Laine. Then again, *her* life had been a little unusual in the past couple of weeks, too. Who knew she'd have fallen ass over elbows in love with a homeless musician?

Realizing Laine was awaiting an answer to her invitation, Cat cleared her throat. "I—sure I'll be there. Where else you gonna get a maid of honor?"

"No kidding?"

"No kidding. Maybe I'll even have a date to bring with me. Someone special."

This time, Laine was the one who sounded surprised. "Really?"

"Yeah," she admitted softly. But she didn't elaborate. This phone call was about Laine's upcoming wedding, not Cat's, uh…*wild and crazy fling. Just a wild and crazy fling.*

Maybe if she told herself that often enough, she'd actually start to believe it.

But probably not.

After her sister had filled her in on the details, Cat realized she had some quick plans to make. Flying to Georgia for one night wasn't going to be easy...particularly not during Temptation's final weekend in business! That her sister would even schedule her impromptu wedding for this weekend told her how completely out of her mind in love Laine must be.

Not wanting to bring her down, Cat didn't mention the bar or the fact that this would be the last Saturday night they'd ever be open. It was definitely a hardship. But there was no place else she'd rather be than at Laine's side on her wedding day.

"I still can't believe you're doing this," she said with a shocked laugh. "Does Mom know?"

"Yes, and she's coming." Laine went on to give her more details.

"Okay, I got it," she said, scratching down the information on a crumpled napkin. "Saturday the twenty-fifth, you can count on me."

Even as she made mental plans, she acknowledged that her relationship with her sister was changing, likely forever. She wanted that relationship to be a positive one. An open, honest one, particularly if Laine was gonna end up living in another state. "Maybe we can find a few minutes to talk," she said, holding tightly to the phone cord for courage. "A lot's been going on with me, too. I'm thinking about going back to college. I even have all the paperwork filled out."

"Wow." Laine paused for a second, then added, "Then the bonus money I earned for the cover of *Century* is going to come in handy."

Her sister's dreams really were coming true. Cat knew

how much this meant for Laine's career. "You got the cover? Really?"

"Yep. And it's definitely enough for tuition."

Cat immediately refused. "You keep the money...start a college fund for your first baby." Then something occurred to her, "Oh, God, you're not pregnant, are you?"

Laine laughed. "Definitely not."

"Okay, because one bit of wild, impulsive Laine news per day is my quota," Cat said. Knowing her sister, she stressed, "As for the money, I mean it, I'll be fine. I think the two of us are going to come out a little better than we expected on the furniture and fixture sales."

Her voice soft, Laine said, "You've been amazing the last couple of weeks, you know? I felt so overwhelmed when I left, as if everyone was relying on me to fix everything."

That hurt a little, since Cat had wanted so much from her sister—*except* fixing. "If you'd wanted out, all you had to do was say so."

"No, I couldn't. Temptation meant too much to you and Mom."

Yeah, it had. Whether she'd ever realized it before or not, she had to admit that her sister had made some sacrifices to help Cat keep the business up and running.

Laine added, "And don't worry about the closing. I'll be back to help with that."

"Seriously, you don't need to. I've got everything under control." Well, that was something of a whopper considering her personal life was about as out of control as it had ever been, but she meant it about the business. There was nothing Laine could do here and she didn't need to be brought down by dealing with it.

"Really? You're not just saying that?"

"No. I'm not. But is there any chance you can make a pit

stop here before you guys go on your honeymoon? I'd love for you to be here for the party on Monday, after we officially close. I think Mom's even considering hopping a flight and coming…which means you gotta be here to referee."

"I wouldn't miss that for the world," Laine replied with a laugh. Then, after the slightest hesitation, she murmured, "And Cat, just in case you change your mind, remember, I'm always here if you need me."

Hearing the verbal olive branch, Cat reached out and grabbed it. "I know you are. You always have been." Then, smiling a little, she added, "I'll see you Saturday."

WHEN DYLAN ARRIVED back at Temptation Thursday afternoon, he found Cat involved in a flurry of activity. She was barking something over her shoulder at Zeke, who stood in the doorway to the kitchen, a laconic look on his grizzled face.

Cat's friend Vicki—who'd waited tables a few weekends ago—was back. She stood beside Dinah, nodding as Cat pointed at some signs and flyers strewn across the bar. Beside Cat was an older man, stoop-shouldered and white-bearded. He was paying careful attention to every word she said. Actually, judging by where most of the old geezer's attention was focused, he was paying much more careful attention to Vicki's legs, revealed by her skimpy jean shorts.

Dylan rolled his eyes, smothering a laugh. Then he realized what Cat was telling the old man: she was teaching him how to make a drink. When she reached for the familiar bottle of Irish Cream, Dylan coughed into his fist, wondering if she was telling him how to make the concoction Dylan had consumed off Cat's body the other night.

"You're back!" she said, her entire face lighting up with her smile.

God, that smile. He could live on that and nothing else and never want for anything. "I'm back," he said, ambling across the room. He reached into his pocket and dug out a bank envelope, then slapped it onto the bar. "That antique dealer went nuts over those two old pinball machines you said have been here since Prohibition. And he loved the old carousel horse, too."

Cat's eyes lit up. "Really?" When she reached for the envelope and started counting cash, shock washed over her face. "*This* nuts?"

Well, maybe not *that* nuts. Maybe Dylan had kicked in a little extra, but still, the antiques had commanded a good price. "There's a small fortune in the *junk* that broker so graciously offered to *take off your hands* for next to nothing."

"No kidding." She came out from around the bar and threw her arms around his neck, giving him a big loud kiss right in front of the others. "One more reason to be very thankful you came walking through my door two weeks ago, Dylan Spence."

"It's Spencer," he murmured, suddenly realizing he'd never clarified his full name for her.

"I should have figured," she said. Then she kissed him again and tried to step away. "Thanks again, Dylan Spencer."

Wrapping his arms around her waist, he held her close, not letting her pull away. "I'm glad I could be here to help. And I'll be right here until the last chair is paid for and the last light fixture carefully packed."

Her clear green eyes shifted away, as if his words had bothered her instead of reassuring her. "Cat?"

"You two gonna make out all day or finish teaching me how to make these girlie drinks?" the old-timer at the bar said, sounding as amused as he did surly.

"Sorry, Uncle Ralph," she said as she stepped out of

Dylan's arms, then made the introductions. "Dylan, this is my uncle Ralph, who used to run the bar with my mom. He retired without ever learning the finer points of, uh…froufrou drinks."

Lowering his voice, he asked, "Hmm, does he know how to make a Slippery Nipple?"

"What was that?" her uncle Ralph asked. "Did he say what I thought he said?"

Dinah and Vicki were both grinning, neither of them stepping up to explain.

"No, he didn't," Cat said. Leaning up on tiptoe to kiss Dylan's cheek, she whispered, "He hears better than my mother did when I tried to sneak in after my curfew."

He laughed, as she'd intended him to, but after the way she'd said his full name for the very first time a moment ago, the image of Cat as a teenager made him edgy. If she started putting two and two together…she might come up with a rat.

Namely him.

This was getting crazy. He had to come clean. Every day that went by brought them closer to the end of her life here at Temptation, and closer to her future. A future he very much wanted to share.

So why haven't you told her?

There were a number of reasons, really. There was still work to do. Plus, he suspected Cat would need him emotionally after she locked the door for the last time after the last customer.

Oh, and there was the fact that he was a chickenshit.

He didn't want to lose her. Didn't want to see her face tighten with dismay—or, even worse, indifference—when she realized there was about as much chance of him riding out of here on that Harley as there was of old Uncle Ralph there ever learning how to make froufrou drinks.

"So why the hands-on training?" he asked, watching Cat walk back around the bar to rejoin her uncle.

"Uncle Ralph's going to cover for me Saturday night."

Sliding up onto one of the stools, Dylan gave her a curious look. "What's Saturday night?"

"I have to go out of town."

His jaw almost hit the bar. Cat was leaving town—leaving *him*—the day after tomorrow? Right in the middle of her last weekend in business? "You gotta be kidding me."

Cat shrugged. "No choice. Family comes first."

Oh, no, someone in her family was hurt. Sick. That was the only possible explanation. He felt like a first-class heel for his flash of dismay, which had been so selfish when Cat was in the midst of a family crisis. "I'm so sorry. Is it bad?"

"It's totally insane."

Very bad. "I'll help cover the bar. Anything you need."

Cat blinked, looking surprised. Then a hint of color rose in her cheeks. "I'd kind of hoped you might come with me."

He didn't hesitate, glad she'd want him by her side during a family tragedy. Because that's exactly where he most wanted to be. "Of course. Anywhere."

"Great. Do you...I hate to ask this, but do you have a suit?"

A *suit*? A dark suit? God, someone had died. "Who..."

"It's Laine."

Laine. Her sister. The photographer chasing wildfires in California. Dylan jumped off his stool and pulled her toward him, tugging her across the bar and into his arms. "God, Cat, honey, I'm so sorry."

Cat wriggled a bit, pulling back so she could look him in the eye. She half lay on the bar, supporting herself on her fists, and gave him a look as if he were totally nuts. "Spence, my sister is getting *married*."

Dylan closed his eyes and counted to ten, to savor his relief and hide his embarrassment at having jumped to a very wrong conclusion. When he opened them, he saw everyone in the room staring at him. "Good God, Cat, I thought you were telling me we were going to a funeral!"

Cat's eyes widened into twin circles, then she nibbled her lip. "Sorry, I guess I'm a little scatterbrained. It's been kinda crazy ever since she called and told me she's getting married Saturday, in Georgia."

"Georgia? Your sister is getting married *this* weekend, in another state?"

Cat probably heard the indignation in his voice. Judging by the frowns on the faces of the others in the room, they'd all been wondering the same thing…how could her sister have forgotten—or ignored—what this weekend meant to Cat?

"She's crazy in love," Cat explained with a helpless shrug. "And you know what? More power to her." She looked around the room, at the bare walls, the space where the pinball machines had stood, then back at him. "If I'd stayed here, I would have been moping and sad and worried. This way, I have something wonderful and bright and beautiful to do on Saturday instead of crying in my beer about something I simply cannot change."

There was genuine honesty in her expression, and that excited smile still tugged at her beautiful lips. She obviously meant it. Which made him believe that, at last, Cat really was preparing to let go of the bar for good. That she was already looking forward to the future. Laine's…and possibly her own.

"Okay," he said. "I can manage a suit. When do we leave?"

"I plan to look into airfares right after I reach the liquor supplier, who I've been trying to call all morning." She put a hand up, stopping him before he could say a word. "And I *will* be paying for your ticket. You're doing me a favor by coming as my date, and since you're not letting me pay you, this'll make me feel better. Even though the amount I'll spend would be slave wages in comparison to the hours you've worked, especially since I've earned so much more than I would have if you hadn't been around."

He wasn't going to have this argument again, not in front of the others, especially. But soon—once he'd come clean to her about his real situation, including his finances—he'd make sure she let him pay her back. "You're on. So we'll be back here by Sunday for the official closing day?"

She nodded, rattling off the details. "I figured we'd fly out Saturday morning and back Sunday morning. Dinah, Vicki, Zeke and Uncle Ralph can cover Saturday night. We'll be here for one final day with the customers Sunday afternoon and evening. And then we'll have our big final private party on Monday."

She had everything figured out. Typical Cat...got knocked by some completely unexpected surprise and just rolled right with it. As always, she amazed him. "Sounds like a plan."

Vicki cleared her throat. "Uh, Cat, what liquor supplier do you use?"

"Texas Todd's," she murmured, already reaching for the phone. "Though, if they're going to be this unreliable, I might have to rethink that, which could be tough since they're the only supplier within sixty miles of here."

"Uh-oh," Vicki said softly. "Have you been watching the news or reading the paper at all this week?"

"No. I've been kind of busy. Why? What is it?" Cat asked as she slowly returned the telephone receiver to its cradle and gave her friend her full attention.

Seeing tiny, tense lines appear around Cat's mouth, he knew she was preparing to be hit by yet another crisis. Hit hard. Dylan stiffened. What, exactly, was about to land on Cat's shoulders now?

"I hate to tell you this," Vicki said, her reluctance evident in her tone, "but something happened at the Texas Todd's warehouse here in Kendall Sunday night. They said on the news that a bad wire sparked a fire that turned into an enormous blaze. The whole place went up in smoke. It was completely destroyed."

They were all silent for a moment, looking at the nearly drained bottles on the half-empty shelves. Dylan breathed deeply as the truth slowly sank in. Even if Cat could find another supplier in Texas close enough to stock her up in time for this weekend, what company would want to deliver to a bar that was closing the next day? He knew enough about the law to know there was a lot of paperwork and a ton of regulations governing businesses that sold liquor, and she'd have to jump through a lot of hoops with a brand-new company. That would take time. Time Cat simply didn't have.

Judging by the shock and dismay on everyone's faces, they'd all come to pretty much the same conclusion. But nobody spoke, not until her Uncle Ralph cleared his throat. "Well," he said, sounding philosophical, "Guess that means I don't have to learn how to make any froufrou drinks after all."

Cat didn't say a word. She simply turned on her heel and stalked out of the bar.

SITTING IN A CHAIR by the window overlooking the back garden, Cat stared outside, deep in thought. She still couldn't quite believe it. She'd been all ready to close down after this weekend, somehow making herself believe she was totally okay.

But now…now the end had come and she hadn't even prepared herself for it. If they didn't run out of booze tonight, they would by tomorrow night. Meaning no matter what, Temptation was officially out of business in a little over twenty-four hours.

She didn't cry. Her eyes didn't even well up. Instead, she sat at the window, looking down at the greenery her grandmother had planted and tended two decades before. At the limestone wall she used to climb as a kid, when her parents were inside working and her older sister was off studying…being the angel.

Cat had spent most of her childhood here, with a family who worked 24/7 on their business. She'd knocked out her first tooth when she'd fallen off a stool by the bar. She'd come here after school every day growing up, doing her homework in the kitchen while her grandmother made the Irish stew Sheehan's Pub used to be famous for.

Her first date had picked her up downstairs, under the watchful eye of her parents and Uncle Ralph. Here's where she'd had her first job…her only job. And here's where they'd held the Irish wake for her dad, which had drawn more than three hundred people and had gone on all night.

Lots of memories. Lots of ghosts.

Still dry-eyed, Cat finally began to realize something. It wasn't the bar—or the *building* she was going to miss. It wasn't the customers or the smell or the sounds or the excitement. It wasn't the freedom or the fun or the music.

It was the past. She'd held on so tightly to this place because it linked her to the past and to the people who'd meant so much to her, who'd all drifted away. As if she could somehow keep them close by holding on to the place where they'd last been together.

Where she'd last seen their faces.

"You don't love working this bar," she whispered, knowing it was true. She just hadn't known any other way to live. And she'd thought that by staying here, she was keeping the whole family alive. But now, knowing she'd soon be leaving here for the last time, she began to accept that all those memories and moments she'd been so afraid of losing were going to be leaving with her.

"Cat?" she heard from behind her.

Spence. He'd entered so quietly she hadn't even known he'd followed her up to her apartment.

"Hey."

"You okay?"

She nodded. "Yeah. I am." Forcing a laugh, she added, "At least now, I won't have to worry about missing work Saturday. I don't suppose we'll have anything to serve by last call tonight."

He squatted beside her chair, looking so worried, so concerned. The warmth in his brown eyes and the tenderness in his stare got to her. Really got to her, way down deep.

She in no way wanted to let this man get away. Because she loved him. Truly loved him, no matter what she'd been trying to tell herself. Cat would sooner strike a match and fling it at the bottles of liquor downstairs than let this man walk out of her life. "I'm so glad you're here," she finally said. "You've made this bearable, you know?"

"Is there anything else I can do?"

Reaching toward his long, silky hair, she ran her fingers through it, then offered him a shaky smile. "Help me make some Drink Till We're Dry signs?"

He laughed softly. Turning his head until his face curved against her hand, he gently kissed her palm.

"Will you do something else for me, Spence?"

"Anything."

Thinking about tonight, about Temptation going out in style, she asked, "Will you play tonight? Just you, with your guitar, play like Temptation's the *Titanic* and you're the orchestra?"

He didn't even hesitate. "Absolutely."

Smiling, she gave him a grateful nod.

"Will you do something for me, too?" he asked. "Tomorrow, when this is all over, will you come somewhere with me? I have something I want to show you…something I want to talk to you about. I think we should get some things out in the open."

Cat was, of course, curious, but her mind was already caught up in how to get the word out about tonight. She had calls to make, signs to print up. The word would spread quickly, she knew, she just needed to get it started.

Yeah, there was definitely a lot to do…but a big part of her wanted to just stay here for a little while longer. With him.

"Cat? What do you say? Can we talk tomorrow?"

She nodded. "Sure. But for right now…"

"Yes?"

Sliding out of her chair, she knelt in front of him on the carpet, then wrapped her arms around his neck. "Right now, I want you to make love to me." Pressing her lips to his, she kissed him, mentally telling him all the things she'd realized but hadn't yet figured out how to put into words.

In silence, Spence rose, drawing her with him. Cat didn't even try to protest when he bent and lifted her into his arms, carrying her the short distance back to her bedroom. When he gently laid her on the bed, she drew him down with her, feeling weak and hungry, empty and ful-filled, all at the same time.

As always, Spence seemed to know exactly what she needed and how she needed it. In recent days, they'd made love in a lot of ways, a lot of moods. Crazy and wild and hot and intense.

But this time, it was incredibly sweet.

Kissing her deeply, he slowly drew her clothes off her body, stroking and caressing every inch as it was revealed. He focused all of his attention on pleasuring her. His every touch was delightful, every kiss intoxicating. All her nerve endings sparked and sizzled, until she could barely breathe because of the sensations washing over her.

"You're gonna be okay, Cat," he whispered as he pulled away long enough to take off his own clothes.

"I know."

Cupping her face in his hand, he stared into her eyes, then slowly entered her. Cat curved up, welcoming him, meeting his slow, deliberate thrusts, wondering how she'd ever thought she'd known anything about lovemaking before she met this man.

Sliding in and out of her with sweet hunger and passion, Dylan kissed her forehead, her temple, her eyelids. The beauty of it moved her, called to her and eventually overwhelmed her. For the first time in months, Cat gave in to the emotion, to the feelings battering her from all directions, knowing she was in the arms of a man who adored her and would keep her safe.

And finally, she let go. Let go of everything. Including her long-unshed tears.

DYLAN HADN'T PERFORMED *alone* in front of an audience in a long, long time. But somehow, Thursday night, it seemed easy. Maybe because, in spite of the crowd who'd gathered to say goodbye to Temptation, he always kept his focus on Cat.

She looked beautiful. Deciding to live up to the name of her establishment, she'd dressed all in vivid, hot, tempting red. Every guy in the place was drooling, but Cat's body language made it clear she was taken. By him.

He hoped she'd still feel that way tomorrow because he was going to come clean with her. Everything had to be out in the open *before* he went with her to her sister's wedding.

He simply couldn't put it off, couldn't go mingle with her family and stand by her side when he'd been lying to her for weeks. So he planned to take her out to his house and get everything out in the open. And then ask her to live in it with him. As his wife.

He definitely wasn't lying tonight. As he went through his repertoire of torchy rock songs on the stage, he really sang only to Cat. The rest of the crowd faded to insignificance, just background chatter. He was giving her what she'd asked for, entertaining her customers, but every heated word of every hot song was directed entirely at the woman tending bar. Particularly when he dug all the ones he'd written for her out of his brain.

Including one he'd been working on for the past several days. Called "In The Garden," it was something he'd been playing around with in private. He'd never had any intention of performing it, certainly not this soon after writing it. But just in case the bottom dropped out of his world tomorrow, and she decided she liked the biker, not the software engineer, he wanted to make sure she knew how he felt.

As soon as he sang the first few words, he knew he had her attention. Cat's head jerked, and she stared at him from across the room. Slowly lowering the bottle she'd been pouring from, she froze, standing in utter stillness, listening to the words.

He only hoped she remembered them tomorrow.

After it was done, she gave him an intimate smile that told him she understood—and appreciated—every word.

After he'd sung his third set, late in the night, he lowered his guitar, needing a drink and a break. It was nearly closing time, and, as Cat had predicted, they'd run out of most of their drinks earlier in the evening. But people were sticking around, wanting the friendship and the camaraderie to last a bit longer.

Making his way across the room, he accepted the thanks from the audience, saying his goodbyes to the regulars he'd come to know in recent weeks. But he never took his eyes off his target, who was watching his progress out of the corner of her eye.

"That was amazing," Cat said as soon as he slid up onto the only vacant stool at the bar. "The garden song…wow." He didn't know if it was the reddish glow from the lights, or a reflection off her devil-red blouse, but he'd swear her cheeks held a hint of a blush. "Did you…write that recently?"

Accepting a bottle of water from her, he nodded, then gave her an intimate smile. "Yeah. Very recently."

The color in her face grew deeper. Dylan couldn't contain a small chuckle. "I don't think I've ever seen you blush before."

"Yeah, well, don't get used to it. I only like red from the neck down."

He sat there with her for another half hour, as the crowd finally started to drift away. It was a work night, after all. Cat accepted tons of hugs and her tip jar looked ready to explode. Soon there were just a handful of people left, including Vicki, Dinah, Ralph and Zeke, all of whom were sitting at the bar, nursing their own bottles of beer, which Zeke had kept stashed in the kitchen fridge.

"This was great, Cat. Man, I'm really gonna miss this place," he heard someone say.

That comment had come from a guy behind him. Glancing over his shoulder, he saw a stranger, a young man, who gave Cat a friendly smile. "Girl, it's a damn good thing you called me to come work on that bike this afternoon, or I wouldn't known about tonight's closing-down party."

Casting a quick glance at Cat, he saw her eyes grow wide. "Uh, glad you could make it," she mumbled.

Dylan tensed, a sense of foreboding putting him on edge.

"But, you know, it's not like I could do anything," the stranger said, keeping his voice loud to be heard over the last of the crowd lingering nearby. Shouldering his way closer, until he stood directly beside Dylan, he added, "There's not a thing I could do with that Harley. She's a beauty, well-maintained, and purrs like a kitten. Don't know why you thought there was something wrong with her." Then he tossed a familiar-looking set of keys onto the bar, which he hadn't seen since he put them in the grungy duffel bag he'd gotten from Banks.

Damn. This guy was talking about Jeremy's motorcycle. No doubt about it. "Cat…"

"What do you mean it's running?" she asked sharply, looking back and forth between the stranger and Dylan. Her eyes narrowed. "You told me it was broken-down."

"You called a mechanic?" was all he could manage to sputter, instantly put on the defensive.

"Because you wouldn't let me pay you."

"Because I don't accept money from women I'm sleeping with," he shot back.

The stranger whistled. "Okay, I'm outta here."

Everyone else within earshot seemed much less considerate. The conversation at the bar seemed to drop to a dull drone.

Cat seemed to realize they'd drawn a lot of attention, too. Looking around frantically, she gestured toward her uncle Ralph. The old man nodded at her signal and came around to relieve her, though, with closing time just five minutes away, he wouldn't have much to do.

Focusing on Dylan, she muttered, "Let's go."

Trying to figure out how to explain, he followed her out of the bar and up the stairs to her apartment. Things were coming to a head a little sooner than he'd planned, and definitely not in the *way* he'd planned. Cat was already tense and upset. He just hoped he wasn't about to make things much, much worse.

"You lied to me about the motorcycle not running," she said as soon as they entered her apartment.

Kicking the door shut behind him, he nodded. "Yeah."

She crossed her arms. "Why?"

He thought it over, wondered what to say, then finally realized nothing would do but the truth. The whole, entire, lame-ass truth.

So that's exactly what he told her.

10

HE WASN'T a homeless musician. HE wasn't a starving songwriter. He didn't ride a Harley and he didn't usually wear scruffy jeans and hard-rock-band T-shirts. He didn't live a carefree life and he didn't like to travel the world, being tied down to nothing and answerable to no one.

If she were just meeting him, Spence would be the man of her mature, grown-up Catherine Sheehan dreams. But she hadn't just met him. And she was still just Cat.

"You lying son of a bitch."

Spence's eyes widened slightly, but he didn't speak up in his own defense.

"You mean to tell me you have a car parked down the block? And you own a house in Tremont?"

"Yes."

"You…you're a software engineer of all things?"

He shoved his hands into his jean pockets. Through the thin, worn fabric, she could see them curling into fists. "Yes."

Still not quite believing it, Cat just shook her head, then slowly lowered herself onto her sofa, pulling her legs up in front of her. Wrapping her arms around them, she stared at him, trying to make sense of it all.

He'd faked being some broke, starving musician, living here and working like a dog for weeks. All the while, he'd had a house in what Cat knew was one of the priciest areas around. "Were you just playing a twisted game with me?"

"No game. You needed help. And I wanted to give it to you."

"That's ridiculous. You let me think you were some kind of unemployed laborer looking for work."

"I don't mind real labor, Cat." Pulling his hands out of his pockets, he stepped closer and sat down in a chair opposite her. He dropped his elbows onto his knees and leaned closer. "You needed help. I knew, deep down, that you wouldn't take my help if you didn't think I needed the job. Was I wrong?"

Still glaring, she stuck out her chin and refused to answer.

"That Sunday night…the night we danced on the bar…"

"Don't even go there," she snapped.

He ignored her. "That night, Banks made up that bullshit story about me needing a place to crash and not having a ride."

"Yeah, he did. I suppose he thought it was terribly funny."

"In his own, twisted way, he was trying to help me. Trying to give me a chance with you. I guess we'd both figured that once the Four G's finished playing that weekend, I wouldn't have any excuse to see you again."

She would have found a reason, but she didn't say that. "But *after* he made up all those lies, you went along with them."

"I was about to tell you the truth, but when I opened my mouth to, you started talking about how much you really *did* need help. I thought if you knew the truth you'd politely thank me for the offer, push me out, then try to do everything by yourself."

Yeah, she probably would have. Rubbing a weary hand over her eyes, she admitted it. "You might be right."

"I didn't want to lie to you. But I didn't want to leave, either. And if making you think I needed *you* as much as you needed *me* gave me a chance to see what could happen between us, that was more reason to go for it."

The truth continued to swirl around in her brain, so darned convoluted and yet so simple. When she thought about it, it was funny in an awful, twisted way.

She'd originally decided to steer clear of Spence because she'd thought he was a reckless, broke musician.

Then she'd plunged into an affair with him *because* she'd thought he was a reckless, broke musician.

Now that she knew he wasn't, she had absolutely no idea what she was going to do.

"You know, I'd told myself before you walked into Temptation that first night that I wasn't going to get involved with any more dangerous guys. You seemed a walking, living, breathing example of the kind of man I needed to steer clear of."

"But you changed your mind."

"Yeah. When Banks spun his story about you being the free-spirited drifter I'd imagined you were, I decided I'd have a wild fling with you before you rode away forever. Then I'd settle down and find someone serious and responsible to build a future with."

His jaw tightened. "A wild fling. That's what you wanted?"

She nodded. "That Sunday night when you offered to stay, I'd made the decision to seduce you."

"Because you thought I'd be good for a fling. No strings, no future, nobody you could ever really fall for."

That wasn't quite the way she'd been thinking. At least, she hoped not. Because it sounded awfully hard when spoken out loud like that.

"And now that you know I'm not, you still gonna shove me out of your life and go on to someone mature, responsible and serious?" He rose to his feet, thrusting a frustrated hand through his hair. "This is too damned confusing. You want me for one thing, then for something completely different. How the hell am I supposed to know what you really want? Do *you* even know?"

She leapt to her feet, too. "Well, how am I supposed to know who you really *are* when you haven't been honest with me since the minute you walked through my door?"

Tension snapped between them, as sharp and wicked as a live wire. Cat sucked in a deep breath, trying to remain calm, when she really wanted to smack him for not being who she'd thought he was. And for being exactly who she'd once thought she wanted.

Her head hurt.

"You want to know who I am?" he finally said, his voice thick and ragged. "I'll tell you."

He stepped closer, grabbing her shoulders and holding her steady. "I'm Dylan Spencer. The geeky little teenager you saved from annihilation in a school cafeteria more than nine years ago. The guy who fell a little in love with you right then and there. The one who went completely nuts over you one night when you stared into the flickering light of a bonfire."

Cat froze, having a hard time taking his words in. Was she really hearing what she *thought* she was hearing? She'd *known* him? He'd been a classmate? "You're saying we went to school together?" she asked, completely dumbfounded.

"For one year. I was a senior and you were in tenth grade. You barely noticed me…I didn't exist for you. Too boring, too nondescript, too *normal*." His fingers tightening, he added, "But you definitely existed for me."

Shocked, Cat remained completely speechless. She had no idea what to say. She hadn't recognized him. Lord, she *still* didn't recognize him.

"It's okay, I know you don't remember me. There's no real reason you would. Ours paths almost never crossed, we never officially met." With a small laugh devoid of humor, he added, "And I've changed a whole lot more than you have."

As if realizing he'd been squeezing her hard, he released his grasp on her shoulders and stepped back. Shaking his head, he mumbled something under his breath, then turned on his heel, walking away from her.

"Wait, Spence, you…I don't understand this."

He paused. "Look," he said, not turning around to face her. "You want to know the real reason, the *main* reason I lied to you about who I really am?"

"Yes. I do."

His body straightened, his shoulders squaring, but still he didn't turn around. Cat's breath caught in her throat as she waited for something—some explanation that would make sense of all this.

In a low voice that she almost didn't recognize, he spoke again. "It's because I didn't want to see your eyes glaze over with boredom when you realized I wasn't the kind of guy who'd ever interest you." He paused, then spoke again. "I didn't want to be invisible to you again."

Cat's pulse raced and a roaring sound began to echo in her brain. Good Lord, this man thought he could ever be *invisible* to her? "Spence…"

"It's Dylan," he bit out. "Josh and Banks are the only ones who call me Spence." Striding to the front door, he put his hand on the knob. Before turning it, he finally glanced at her, his expression somber, his eyes hooded. "I'm sorry I lied to you, Cat. I'm truly sorry."

Opening the door, he began to step through it. But before walking out completely, he said one more thing. Something that made time stand completely still.

"And Cat? It was you. The girl with the flames turning her hair to gold and the fire in her eyes? It was you. It's *always* been you."

Then he walked out.

AS IF IT WASN'T BAD ENOUGH that his relationship with Cat had just been blown all to hell, Dylan arrived home Thursday night to find his house trashed. Jeremy had apparently had his party. And considering the teen and two of his buddies were sprawled in lawn chairs by Dylan's pool, it hadn't ended yet.

Staring in disbelief at the stains on his carpets, the hole in the family-room wall and the broken lamp, he bellowed, "Jeremy Garrity, what the hell did you do to my house?"

The three guys launched out of their chairs and raced inside. Jeremy's face paled when he saw the fury in Dylan's. "You're home early."

"No shit, Sherlock." Glaring at the other two guys, he snapped, "Get to work or get out."

The two of them raced for the door, leaving so fast, Dylan barely had time to make a mental note of their faces.

"I'm sorry, man, I guess it got kinda out of hand. I cleaned almost everything up, just had this little bit left to do," Jeremy said weakly.

Almost everything? Shaking his head in disbelief, Dylan simply stared at the young man. Somehow, though, he couldn't muster up much righteous anger. It had simply dissipated. Because what the hell did a couple of stains and broken things matter in comparison to the mess he'd made of his life?

He'd lost her. He'd lost Cat for good. Not only because he wasn't the man she wanted, but because he'd lied to her. *Rat-brained moron.*

But even as a part of him mentally kicked himself, another part of Dylan couldn't stop thinking about Cat's own confession. She'd considered him good enough for a wild fling—and nothing else.

That rankled. So maybe it was just as well she hadn't forgiven him for his deceptions and asked him to stay in her life. Because, at this point, he couldn't be entirely sure whether she wanted *him*, Dylan Spencer, or the phantom responsible, grown-up man she'd told herself she had to find.

"A buddy of mine has a brother who does drywall work," Jeremy said. He was bending down to pick up a few pieces of trash, as well as some of his clothes, which were strewn over the furniture. "He's coming out to fix the hole tomorrow."

"Forget it," Dylan said, rubbing a weary hand over his eyes.

Jeremy straightened and met Dylan's stare unflinchingly. "No, it was my responsibility. I'll pay to get it fixed."

Judging by the young man's earnest expression, he meant what he said. Dylan agreed and gave one short nod. "Your motorcycle's still parked where you left it. Cat has the keys."

The young man grinned. "So did it work? Is she all yours?"

Unable to contain a bitter laugh, he merely walked away.

Eventually, after cleaning up everything he could, Jeremy packed up his stuff and took off. Dylan barely noticed. He'd been locked in the spare room, where he stored his musical equipment.

Music always calmed him, evened him out. The harder the tune, the cooler he got. So by late Thursday night, he was rocking the walls off his house. And he kept rocking them, throughout most of the night, wondering if his neighbors were gonna call the cops, but not really caring.

Taking a break on Friday, he kept his mind off Cat for a while by checking his mail, paying his bills and getting in touch with a company he was supposed to do some programming for. But by that night, he was back in the studio, playing his guitar, his Fender or his keyboard, trying to work through his emotions the way he'd *always* worked through them.

By Saturday, he finally began to feel back in control. Somewhat sane, at least. He'd done a lot of thinking—about the deceptions and the misunderstandings. Her words, and his own.

One thing was clear: they couldn't end things like this.

He loved Cat. He wasn't about to let her go without one more shot at making her believe that. Equally important, he truly believed she loved him. Or, at least, she loved the Spence she'd spent the past two weeks with.

So if he had to become that man to get her back, then by God, that's exactly what he'd do.

CAT THOUGHT SHE'D DONE a darn fine job of hiding her unhappiness during her whirlwind trip to Georgia. She'd smiled and talked and teared up during Laine's wedding to her beaming groom, Steve. She hadn't fought with her mother and had enjoyed getting to know Steve's family.

And she'd somehow managed not to break down and cry one single time. At least, not while anyone was around.

In private, she'd cried a lot.

But something happened Saturday night while she

stood in the shadows, watching Laine dance with her husband, beaming up at him with happiness so bright it blinded. She realized she had been looking at Dylan the same way all week. Finding out that he'd been less than honest about his real life hadn't diminished her feelings. It had angered her, but it hadn't made her miserable.

No. What had made her miserable was the thought that she'd lost him. Really truly lost him. Exactly at the moment she'd started to realize just how long she'd *had* him.

He'd fallen for her years ago when she'd been a flighty, silly high-school girl who hadn't even realized he existed. Maybe it had been a mere teenage infatuation, though, given the intensity of the beautiful song—the song he'd unbelievably written for *her*—she suspected it was something more. It didn't really matter. Because he'd most definitely fallen in love with her during the weeks they'd just spent together. Just as surely as she'd fallen in love with him.

So what the hell was she doing in Georgia, when he was back in Texas, probably wondering if she was ever going to talk to him again? "I need to go home," she whispered to no one in particular. "Now. Right now."

Which is what she did. Despite the fact that the reception was still going strong, Cat slipped away and headed straight for the airport.

Her flight home wasn't until early Sunday morning, but she managed to get a late Saturday night one instead. Before taking off, she'd made a quick cell phone call to Vicki, who did some quick research for her on the Internet. So she now had the home address of a certain Dylan Spencer of Tremont, Texas.

The plane was on the ground in Austin by 3 a.m. and by five, she was back at Temptation, trying to decide whether to go straight to his place now, or go upstairs and catch a couple of hours of sleep first. Knowing she wouldn't be able to sleep until she'd seen his face and made sure she could salvage their relationship, she opted to skip the nap.

The drive to Tremont wasn't a long one, and she was at the front door of Dylan's big two-story house by the time the sun started spreading its yellow-orange rays above the low-hanging clouds on the horizon. "Now or never," she told herself as she reached for the doorbell. Jabbing it with her finger, she paused, then jabbed again. He'd probably need to be woken up.

Suddenly, the door was yanked open and Dylan stood there, rubbing at his eyes, all scruffy and sleepy, wearing only a pair of tight jeans that he hadn't even bothered to button.

Yum.

"Dammit, the party's over, you're a week late," he snarled.

"I am?"

His head jerked up. "Cat?"

"Yeah. Can I come in?"

He stepped back out of the way, allowing her to enter.

"I like your house."

"I can't believe you're here. The wedding…"

"Was lovely."

"You went?"

"Of course I did. Took a redeye home."

Their chatter was light and pointless and served only to let them both adjust to the reality of the moment.

She was here. This was their last chance. And they couldn't blow it.

Taking a deep breath to work up her nerve, Cat started at the beginning. "Dylan…about high school. I'm so sorry."

"Don't be," he said. "If I'd had any guts at all, I would have actually approached you and introduced myself. You just scared the hell out of me." Shaking his head, he admitted, "Sometimes, you still do."

She smiled a little. "You should have. You were *very* cute." Seeing his look of surprise, she explained. "I dug out my tenth grade yearbook. You were adorable." In her own defense, she added, "But you're right, you looked *nothing* like you do now."

"Late bloomer," he replied. He stepped closer, close enough so she could feel the brush of his bare arm on hers, not to mention the warmth of his body. "What are you doing here, Cat?"

Tilting her head back, she stared into his dark brown eyes. "I came to thank you for the song. It called to me from the very first time I heard it."

As if not even aware he was doing it, he lifted his hand to her arm and began to stroke up and down, putting all her senses on red alert. "You're welcome. Is that the only reason you came?"

Slowly shaking her head, she admitted, "I also came to tell you I forgive you. I don't like being lied to, but I think I can understand why you did it. You planned to tell me Friday, didn't you? That's the big 'talk' you wanted to have? And I suppose this house is what you wanted to show me?"

He nodded. "All of the above."

Yeah. She'd surmised as much. Which made things a little better, anyway.

As they both fell silent, Cat tried to figure out what to say next. Should she just blurt out her feelings? Try to be subtle? Jump on the man and be done with it?

"I forgive you, too," he finally said, still touching her so lightly, so delicately, she thought she'd melt. "For thinking I was only good enough for a fling. Hell, nine years ago, that would have sent me right out of my hormone-flooded mind."

Laughing, as he'd intended her to, she stepped closer, until the tips of her shoes nearly touched his bare toes. Their bodies were close together—so close she could see the way the wiry hairs on his chest moved with every breath she exhaled. Dying to tangle her fingers there, she forced herself to refrain, knowing there was more to be said.

He spoke first. "Yesterday, I decided…"

"Yes?"

Clearing his throat, he continued. "I decided that if it was a fling you wanted, I'd become the man you wanted to have one with. I planned to be at your door when you got home today."

Not sure what he meant, she watched as he reached up and tugged at the small earring decorating his earlobe. It didn't come off. "Oh, my God, you got it pierced."

"Uh-huh."

"You hate needles."

"No kidding. Which meant *this* was a real bitch." He pointed to his upper arm, tilting a little so she could see the splash of color on his skin.

She couldn't help gawking at the small Texas star just below his shoulder. "A tattoo? You really went out and got a tattoo?"

"I was just getting warmed up."

"Tell me you didn't pierce anything else on your body. Stick out your tongue!"

He visibly cringed at the possibility. "No more piercings. But there's something parked in my garage that you probably oughtta see."

What he meant dawned on her almost immediately. "You did *not* buy a motorcycle."

"Not exactly," he said with a small, apologetic shrug. "Cat, I'd intended to, but I just couldn't do it. Because I knew damn well you'd want to ride it and I'd be crazy worried every second. But don't you think it's just as dangerous, just as on the edge, to buy one of those Segway people mover things?"

It took a second for her to figure out what he meant. Then she couldn't help giggling out loud. "Considering you could finance the budget of a small country for what those things cost, I'd say, yeah, buying one is definitely living on the edge."

Laughing with her, he slid his arms around her shoulders and pulled her close to him. Cat burrowed against his chest, inhaling deeply, her body reacting to his familiar scent and his warmth. It had been a lonely two-and-a-half days and she never wanted to be out of his arms that long again.

Dylan touched her hair, running his fingers through it. He kissed the top of her head, then her temple. Finally, his lips brushed her earlobe as he whispered, "I love you Cat."

Tilting her head back so she could look into his eyes, she gave the words right back to him. "I love you too, *Dylan*."

Rising on tiptoe, she pressed her lips to his, kissing him with all the emotion that had been building in her for weeks, silently telling him how much she loved him with every delicate brush of their lips and every lazy stroke of their tongues.

When the kiss ended, Dylan didn't release her from his embrace. "You know, the college is only a twenty-minute drive from here. Much closer than from the apartment you planned to move into next week."

"Oh, yeah?"

He nodded. "It'd save you lots of time. And would be

much more economical…think of the money you'd save on gas."

Dylan was stroking her back, his fingertips trailing a lazy circle just above her bottom, and Cat had a hard time focusing on anything he said. She just wanted him to pick her up and carry her to his bedroom. "Uh hmm."

"You agree?"

To anything. She'd agree to anything as long as he didn't stop those tender touches and the sweet kisses he'd begun pressing on her cheek and the corners of her lips. "Sure."

"Good. We'll just bring your stuff right here."

Blinking, she finally gave him her full attention. "My stuff? Wait, you're asking me to move in with you?"

"Yeah. I am. I know we should wait until you finish school, and I don't plan to interfere with that in any way." Lifting his hand to her chin, he gently tilted her head back so he could meet her eyes. "But I've waited a long time to have you in my life, Cat Sheehan. I don't want to wait any more. I want you in my house every day and in my bed every night. And whenever you're ready, I want my ring on your finger and my baby in your belly."

Her head began spinning as the visions of everything he'd just suggested spun in her mind. All of them perfect and so very, very possible. With a deep, contented sigh and pure happiness in her heart, she said, "Yes."

"To moving in?"

"Yes to everything."

AFTER SPENDING ALL DAY Sunday either in his bed or in his kitchen eating to regain their strength, Dylan finally convinced Cat she didn't have to cancel tomorrow's private closing-down party at Temptation. "You've been looking forward to that more than anything else for the last two weeks. You've gotta do it."

"And what am I going to serve?" she asked, her tone as disgruntled as her expression.

He scooped another spoonful of ice cream out of the container they were sharing on top of his kitchen table. "You could serve cocktail wienies and nobody would care. The point is to be together, not what everyone eats."

She shot him a look of impatience. "I mean to drink. What am I supposed to serve to drink? We're completely dry, remember?"

Holding the spoon up to her lips, he watched her lick off every drop of Chunky Monkey. The wicked things she did with her tongue made him wish they'd brought the ice cream to his bedroom.

He cleared his throat. "I suppose you can be forgiven since you haven't started college yet. But haven't you ever heard of those four wonderful little letters, BYOB?"

Frowning, she said, "I can't invite people to a party and then ask them to bring their own refreshments."

"Yeah. You can. A lot of people will be disappointed if you don't go through with it, including your sister and your mother, both of whom are flying in for this thing tomorrow, right?"

She nodded, growing quiet as she began to think about it. Nibbling her lip, with her brow knitted in concentration, Cat looked utterly adorable. He couldn't help smiling.

"What?" she asked when she noticed his expression.

"You're gonna be a lot of fun as a college student. I think I'm really going to like watching you study every night."

"Ugh. Remind me of the whole studying/test thing again and you might just end up wearing this ice cream."

"Sounds cold…but definitely has possibilities," he said, wagging his eyebrows suggestively.

Laughing, she helped herself to another spoonful, then slowly said, "You really think people won't mind?"

"I'm sure of it, Cat. It's you they want to see and say goodbye to. You and the bar."

Finally, she nodded in agreement, then began making calls. And twenty-four hours later, as they stood amid the crowd of happy people at Temptation and he was proved right, he even managed to *not* say, "I told you so."

"I don't think we had this many people in here the entire last six months we were in business," she said, raising her voice to be heard over the chattering partygoers. "Some of these people are from my grandparents' generation."

Following her stare, he looked around the room, which was packed wall to wall. So many new faces, so many new names. Dylan was having a hell of a time keeping them all straight.

At least he knew a few people. Some, like Earl, had been customers he'd met while working here. Uncle Ralph showed up, of course, with his wife, Jill. Vicki was here. And Zeke and Dinah stood near the old jukebox, their arms around each other's waists. Judging by their intimate smiles, he figured his advice to Dinah to make the first move had worked out rather well.

His own friends had even heard about the party and come by. Banks, Josh and Jeremy were milling through the crowd, always up for a party, even if it was with a bunch of people they hardly knew. But they all liked Cat and, per Banks, had decided to come armed with their instruments to make sure Dylan didn't try to do any more performing on his own.

The three of them had been particularly interested in

Cat's friends. Josh had appeared dejected when he'd heard Gracie, the bookstore owner from next door, was involved with someone.

Most of the others in the crowd, however, were strangers to him. He assumed they were people who'd frequented the place when it was Sheehan's Pub, people who'd known Cat's father and grandparents. They told lots of stories and raised their glasses in a lot of toasts. Hearing them reminisce about the old days, he got a real glimpse into Cat's childhood and began to understand a bit more about why she'd become the woman she was. And why she could sometimes seem so alone, even in a crowd.

She'd almost *had* to become adept at that since her entire childhood had been filled with people—family and strangers alike. She'd found a way to disappear inside herself when she needed to…perhaps by shutting out the world with a book.

Or by gazing into the crackling flames of a bonfire.

Cat's family was easy to remember—her attractive sister wore a just-married smile that shone like a beacon Plus, she had her doting firefighter husband glued to her side. They were so obviously newlyweds, there was no mistaking them for anyone else.

"I hear you're going to be living in sin with my daughter."

Ouch. That was the mother. No mistaking her, either. Brenda was direct, outspoken and a little bossy. But she had that same sparkle in her green eyes—so much like her daughter's—and she'd been a big help from the minute she'd arrived.

"Yes, but only until she'll let me make an honest woman out of her," he replied, meeting her stare evenly.

Brenda crossed her arms. "Are you going to tell me what magic spell you wove to get her to decide to go to college?"

"No magic. Cat did that all on her own. She always had the dream...she just needed the opportunity."

Gazing around the room, looking wistful, Brenda murmured, "Now she has her chance. Nothing tying her down here anymore."

Hearing the regret in the woman's voice, he gave her shoulder a squeeze. "She's always going to have this place in her heart. As well as everyone who ever walked through that door."

Brenda covered his hand with her own and nodded. "That's all that really matters, isn't it? The memories we take with us. Not the place where they were made."

Cat, who had walked up from behind just in time to hear her mother's comment, gave them both a warm smile. "Yes. That's all that really matters."

Cat's sister, Laine, also joined them. "Hear, hear."

Without saying a single word, the three Sheehan women exchanged a long, knowing look. Then, almost in unison, they each lifted their glasses—and their gazes—upward, making a silent toast to something above them. Something long gone but never to be forgotten. By the time they sipped their drinks, he'd swear there were tears in all of their eyes.

Before any of them had a chance to speak, Cat's friend, Tess—who'd arrived in an RV with a guy named Ethan—interrupted the chaos in the room. She had gone up onto the stage and was now speaking into the microphone attached to the karaoke machine. "Can I have your attention, please?"

"Oh, heavens, please tell me she's not going to sing," someone murmured. Looking, he realized it was Gracie—who did, indeed, have some of the prettiest eyes he'd ever seen...next to Cat's. She was giving Cat and Laine a worried look.

"I think this party needs a little music," Tess announced.

Cat groaned. "Oh, cripes, she *is* going to sing."

"Maybe love has improved her voice," Laine said doubtfully.

Once Tess launched into the song, appropriately called "The Party's Over," Cat winced and muttered, "Nope. It hasn't."

Cat, Gracie and Laine all started to smile, then to laugh, as all around them the crowd dutifully listened to Tess sing. Badly. Since they were the first to break into huge, loud applause when she was done, he supposed Tess's singing abilities had been a long-standing joke between them.

"Hey, we have a musical act right here who could play," Laine said, eyeing Dylan speculatively. "Why don't we see exactly what it is about you that made my sister go completely mental."

"Takes one to know one," Cat replied with a knowing stare toward Laine's bridegroom.

"Did I hear a request?" asked Banks, who'd been close enough to overhear. "Just been waiting to be asked." He beckoned for Josh and Jeremy. "You guys up for bringing down the house?"

As they nodded, Dylan looked to Cat for approval. She gave him a wide smile. "If it gets Tess away from the microphone, I'll personally hug every member of the Four G's." Then, tilting her head to one side, she asked, "What does that stand for, anyway?"

Banks and Josh both shot him a warning look, but Dylan was never going to keep anything from Cat again. "The Four Geeks."

Cat's jaw dropped, Tess—who'd just stepped off the stage—snickered. And a few others began to mumble softly.

"Uh, guys?" Jeremy said, looking a little shell-shocked. "Are you serious? Is that what it stands for?"

"Never mind. Let's go get our gear," Dylan said. Then he turned toward the door, leading the others.

"Uh, seriously, guys?"

"Shut up, Jeremy," Banks and Josh said in unison.

Jeremy didn't shut up, of course. He continued to gripe about the name as they set up onstage. Dylan finally told him if he didn't leave it alone, he was going to tell his mother about the wild party Jeremy'd had last weekend. That quieted him down.

Picking up his guitar and stepping to the front of the stage, he turned to the others and mumbled the name of an old Sinatra song. Not their usual stuff, but appropriate, he thought.

Cat was watching from the bar, surrounded by her loved ones. Her mother, her sister, her two best friends. So many others. All of them happy and laughing, building lots more memories to take with them when they walked out the door that final time.

"This one's for all of you," he said into the mike. "For everyone who's loved it here."

Then he slowly began the song, "One For My Baby (And One More For The Road)," never taking his eyes off the woman he loved.

As he reached the chorus, he saw her lips begin to move. Soon, he heard voices, and realized nearly everyone in the room had joined in. Everyone, it seemed, was feeling the magic of this place and giving it a proper farewell.

Which was, after all, no more than Temptation deserved.

After the song, there was a long moment of silence, followed by applause, hugs and tears. Though the party would continue, the goodbyes had been said.

Today had been an especially good way for Cat to say goodbye. Now she was ready to stride into her new life. With him.

The possibilities before them were limitless. He had Cat in his life at last, and together…well, together they were perfect. Magical.

As good as rock and roll.

Epilogue

One Week Later

L ast M onday, during Temptation's last big blowout party, Cat had found time to whisper a request of Laine, Tess and Gracie. Which was why the three of them were here, late in the evening on the Fourth of July, watching her climb over the limestone wall into the back garden behind the building she'd lived in until last week.

"Is it open?" Tess whispered.

Cat tested the window, the one she'd purposely left unlocked when she'd left here for what was supposed to be the final time.

"It is. I'll meet you in a sec."

Climbing through the window, she quickly made her way through the deserted building. She moved easily through the shadows to the front door, not worrying about the near darkness. There was nothing to trip over. Not one piece of furniture, not one chair. Only the built-in mahogany bar sitting upon the bare, scarred wood floor. Everything else had been stripped out by the end of the day on Thursday, when Cat had had to turn over her keys to the city official who'd come to make sure she was out.

She'd counted on them not doing anything with the

building until after the holiday weekend, and she'd been right. Nobody'd even been in to ensure the windows were locked. Lucky for her.

"Come in, quick," she said as she opened the front door to her friends. Like thieves in the night, Laine, Tess and Gracie stealthily crept in to join her, all of them dressed in dark clothing, all of them grinning like fools.

"What if we get caught?" Laine asked as she pulled the door closed behind them, peeking out to see if anyone was nearby.

Gracie nibbled her lip. "Will we get arrested?"

"We won't be here long enough for that," Cat said as she began unpacking items from the backpack she'd brought with her and placing them on the bar. A candle, which she lit. Plus a pitcher and some glasses.

It was time for one last Cosmo, for just the four of them.

"Do you realize it's been a month since we got together and did this?" Gracie asked. "It used to be we never missed a week."

Laine shook her head. "I know. But we're here now, that's what counts." Happy and tanned from her Mexican honeymoon, her sister wasn't seeing the negative side of anything.

For that matter, neither was Cat. "Can you believe the last time we did this, all four of us were single with zero in the way of prospects? Now, we're all either married or shacking up."

"I can't say I'm surprised that you and I are shacking up," Tess said. Jerking her thumb toward Gracie, she added, "But can you believe *this* one is?"

Gracie chuckled. "Gotta walk on the wild side now and then."

"By the way," Cat said as she poured their drinks, "I really like Evan, Ethan and Steve."

"Spence is great, too," Laine said. Then, lowering her voice, she added, "We're all going to be very happy, aren't we?"

That summed things up, really, and all four of them slowly nodded. They *were* going to be happy, though their lives had gone in completely unexpected directions. Laine was moving to Georgia, Tess was traveling the country in an RV. Gracie was going to law school and Cat planning for college.

And they were all in love with amazing men who adored them.

"Life doesn't get much better," Cat murmured.

Even as she said it, she was looking around the empty room that had held so much meaning for her, surprised to realize the sadness was already lessening. Thanks to her friends. Her family. Most of all, thanks to Dylan.

"So no more happy hours for the four of us here at Temptation," Laine said wistfully. "I can't believe the Cosmo Quartet is splitting up. Shall we drink a toast to ourselves?"

Raising a doubtful brow, Tess said, "Yes, on the toast. But Cosmo Quartet? If we're going to give ourselves a cutesy name, we can do better than that."

"Much better," Gracie said as she brought her drink to her lips. "Maybe we could name ourselves after that fifties band, the Temptation Four?"

Snickering, Tess said, "They were two groups. The Temptations, and the Four Tops. And it's still not right."

Cat cleared her throat, already lifting her own drink. "How about…to the Temptresses?"

The others immediately nodded at the perfect description. Softly echoing, "To the Temptresses," they all raised their glasses in a tribute to good friends, good times and true love.

Within a few minutes, after they'd shed a few tears and said their goodbyes, they walked to the exit. Cat carried the candle to light their way and watched the others slip out into the dark night, one by one, until she stood alone in the doorway.

Turning one more time to face the room filled with twenty-one years of happy times, she pressed the picture into the memory album in her mind.

And blew out the candle.

The
Temptation
Years
1984–2005

<u>Autographs</u>

Temptation...
Thanks for the memories.
Barbara Daly

Temptation is and always will be home. The line and its readers gave me my start. I love you all!
Carly Phillips

Temptation always had the heroines I wanted to be — and the heroes I wanted to have!
Cindi Myers

Thanks for the memories, Temptation! And thanks especially for putting me in touch with so many wonderful readers. I'll miss you.
Cara Summers

I'll miss our steamy nights and laughs, always!
Julie McBride

I ♡ Temptations!
I made my Harlequin debut there & found some of my 'fave authors between Temptation covers. Temptresses RULE! ☺
Dawn Atkins

My dear Temptation,
What can I say? You've
given me some wonderful reads,
launched my career, and introduced
me to a whole slew of new friends.
You had a fabulous run and I'll miss you!
Love,
Julie Kenner

It is with great sadness I say goodbye
to Temptation. So many wonderful
stories... so many great authors. Thanks
to editors Brenda Chin and Jennifer Green
for giving me a home, and to the
Temptresses for making me feel so
welcome!

All my best,
Jill Monroe

Dear Temptation,
Thanks for giving this
"nice girl" a chance to be
"just a little bit naughty."
Debbie Blackner

Dear Temptation,
You were the first Harlequin line
I fell in love with as a reader,
and the line I felt honored
to break into as an author.
Colleen Collins

Thanks for my ten tempting years!
Heather MacAllister
June 1995 - June 2005

For all the friends I've made
and stories I've loved -- It was
my pleasure to be led into Temptation
Jacquie D'Alessandro

Thanks for giving me my
start! I'll always be
a "Temptation" writer.
Kate Hoffmann

Dear Temptation--

What a run! As a reader,
I learned anything is
possible if you approach
life with a little sass.

Heck, I learned the same
as a writer.
Here's to sass!
Julie Elizabeth
Leto

"Temptation" was right there at the
start of SEXY and HOT. She'll be
remembered with love and a
quickened pulse by
Barbara Delinsky

My love and undying gratitude
to my readers. I couldn't have
enjoyed seventeen fabulous years
at Temptation without you!
Kristine Rolofson

Temptation will always
have a home on my bookshelf!
KRISTIN GABRIEL

First kiss. First lover. First book.
I'll never forget the Temptation!
Smooches,
Cheryl

My keeper shelf is stuffed
full of Temptation stories
and I've loved every month
of this awesome line! Thanks
for all the great reading :
Joanne Rock

Writing for the Temptation line
helped me to find my voice as
a writer. I'm proud to be
forever linked to this line as
a Temptress! Stephanie Bond

Happy retirement,
Temptation!
You've brought me so
much joy and laughter
through the years. It's
hard to watch you go.
— Wendy Etherington

For years, Temptations were the books I loved to read. Becoming a Temptress was a dream come true and forged lasting friendships with both authors and readers. Thank you, Temptation, for the fun, laughter, and good times!

Janelle Denison

Not only did Temptation give me my start, it also gave me some of the greatest friends of my life. I'll always be honored to have been a Temptress!

Leslie Kelly

Thanks to Harlequin—you let your writers spread their wings and fly.—We've touched the sky.—

Sandra Chastain

Thank you, Temptation, for giving me special friends I'll value for a lifetime. The camaraderie and talent within the line, and the readers who gave it popularity, made writing for Temptation a very special time in my life. I'll miss the fun more than I can say.

Lori Foster

My very first book was a Temptation, so the line will always hold a special place in my heart.

I wish all the talented authors, brilliant editors and, most of all, the faithful readers all the best for the future.

Always a Temptress!
Nancy Warren

There is nothing like diving into a ghost, totally fun story — I have only the best memories of writing for Temptation.
Carla Neggers

From getting that first call for CALL ME on national televisio to being a part of the line's 15th Anniversary... thanks, Temptation, for all of the memories! Alison Kent

Temptation Romances taught me to believe. Not only in the power of love, but also in the power of being a woman. So being published in the line was the ultimate expression of all the things I learned from the line, independence, belief in myself, and faith that success on every level was within my grasp. Thank you HQ for giving women strong, sexy role models to show them the way!

Marie Fox

Hey, sweet Temptation! What a kick
hanging out with you. Thanks for the
memories! XX OO Vicki Lewis Thompson

True love stories never
have endings —
Friends 4-ever!
Jeri & Tom
aka
Tori Carrington

JoAnn Ross

I can resist everything
but Temptations!!
Kathleen
O'Reilly

Blaze™

HARLEQUIN® *Blaze*™

New York Times bestselling author

Elizabeth Bevarly

answers the question

Can men and women have sex and still be friends?

with

INDECENT SUGGESTION
Blaze #189

Best friends Becca and Turner try hypnosis to kick their smoking habit...instead, they get the uncontrollable urge to burn up the sheets! Doesn't that make them more than friends?

Be sure to catch this funny, sexy story available in July 2005!

Blaze™

HARLEQUIN® Blaze™

Where were you when the lights went out?

Shane Walker was seducing his best friend in:

#194 NIGHT MOVES

by Julie Kenner   July 2005

Adam and Mallory were rekindling
the flames of first love in:

#200 WHY NOT TONIGHT?

by Jacquie D'Alessandro   August 2005

Simon Thackery was professing his love...
to his best friend's fiancée in:

#206 DARING IN THE DARK

by Jennifer LaBrecque   September 2005

24 Hours: BLACKOUT

Silhouette®

Desire®

Welcome to Silhouette Desire's brand-new installment of

TEXAS Cattleman's Club

The drama unfolds for six of the state's wealthiest bachelors.

BLACK-TIE SEDUCTION
by Cindy Gerard
(Silhouette Desire #1665, July 2005)

LESS-THAN-INNOCENT INVITATION
by Shirley Rogers
(Silhouette Desire #1671, August 2005)

STRICTLY CONFIDENTIAL ATTRACTION
by Brenda Jackson
(Silhouette Desire #1677, September 2005)

*Look for three more titles from Michelle Celmer,
Sara Orwig and Kristi Gold to follow.*

Silhouette Desire

presents

the final installment of

THREE WAY WAGER

*The Reilly triplets bet they could go
ninety days without sex. Hmm.*

THE LAST
REILLY STANDING
by Maureen Child

(SD #1664, available July 2005)

Aidan Reilly was determined to win the bet
he'd made with his brothers. Three months
without sex meant one thing: spend *a lot* of
time with his best gal pal Terry Evans. She had
given up on love long ago because the pain
just wasn't worth it. Then…temptation proved
to be too much. The last Reilly standing had
lost the bet, but could he win the girl?

Available at your favorite retail outlet.